They Crossed the Line
or Decameron Revisited

James A. Booker

INKWATER PRESS
Portland • Oregon
inkwaterpress.com

Cover and interior design by Joy Uyeno

© Greg Ritchie. DreamsTime.com

www.inkwaterpress.com

ISBN-13 978-1-59299-619-3
ISBN-10 1-59299-619-12

Publisher: Inkwater Press

Printed in the U.S.A.
All paper is acid free and meets all ANSI standards for archival quality paper.

1 3 5 7 9 10 8 6 4 2

Special thanks to CCB

1

Uncle Mac is dead. He was seventy-eight and the last of the four. None of them made it to eighty. I don't think they really expected to. Now that they're all gone, I can tell their secrets. They made me promise to wait until they were no longer living. I kept my word. They would have expected no less from me.

In the summer of 1985, I was right out of college and needed a break before starting my new teaching job. My Uncle Mac seized the opportunity to recruit me as the designated driver on a trip to Alaska. He had just attended a reunion of his police academy class after twenty-five years. Most of them were recently retired from their various law enforcement agencies, and the four of them had decided to take a month off from responsibility, rent a large RV, and drive to Alaska. Since they planned to do some serious beer drinking on the way, it seemed like a good idea to take along a non-drinker to do most of the driving. They offered to cover my expenses, so it sounded like a good deal to me.

The four had a lot in common. It took me a while to recognize their individual differences. Each had served in the military right after the Korean War, although in various branches. Because there had been a lull in the action during the Fifties, none of them had seen any combat. They were all from the Midwest, but no two from the same state. They had enrolled in a police academy in Chicago at the same time and, as cold-war veterans, had found a common bond. They had socialized together, if drinking beer and attending sporting events could be called socializing. They were all big men, since the standard then for police officers required applicants to be at least five-ten. Back then there were no women and few minorities enrolled. It was a different social structure at that time. In some ways, it was a different world from the one I knew.

Here is the cast of characters:

Ben Randall had grown up on a farm in Nebraska and had never been farther away from home than Colorado as a boy. When he graduated from high school, he became enticed by a recruiting poster which read, "Join the Navy and see the world." Feeling venturesome, he enlisted for a four-year commitment and did indeed see a large part of the world, even if most of it was only port cities. After he was discharged, he had no great desire to return to the farm, and somehow he wound up at the police academy in Chicago. I'm not sure why. He was probably the smallest and quietest of the four, but he always seemed confident. After graduation from the academy, he took a job with the state police in Nebraska and got married. Both choices turned out unfavorably for him, and he made a career move to Kansas City after his divorce. A position with the Kansas City police force turned out much better for him, and he was promoted to the rank of lieutenant after several years. He never remarried. It would have been uncharacteristic of him to talk about it. He didn't discuss his private life.

Karl Schultz was a big, bald-headed bear of a man from Milwaukee who delighted in telling jokes and making preposterous claims. He said that he had originated the phrase, "Twenty-four hours in a day. Twenty four beers in a case.

Coincidence?" He further claimed to have demonstrated that it was actually possible on several occasions. He attributed it to his German genes. I watched him come close enough to verifying his boast that I never questioned it. Oddly enough, he never showed any signs of physical or mental impairment, no matter how much beer he drank. He had joined the Army after high school in order to be sent to Germany, where he still had many relatives. While there, he married a German woman named Helga, who later became a nurse and seemed like a stabilizing influence in his life. After completing his service obligation and graduating from the police academy, he and his wife returned to Milwaukee, where he spent his entire career on the police force and she worked in a hospital. She had not shown any interest in accompanying us on our trip, which was probably just as well. On the other hand, we could have used someone who knew how to cook something that didn't come out of a can. I did most of the cooking, as long as it didn't go far beyond frying bacon and eggs or tending the grill.

Bill Roberts was the most athletic of the four. He had been a three-sport letterman at a Kansas high school. He had always wanted to become a policeman because he was supremely confident in his ability to run down and outfight anyone. After high school he had hoped to get a college football scholarship, but it didn't happen. With no alternative plan to finance college, he enlisted in the Army's military police, hoping to be sent to Europe. Instead, he spent a year in Korea and two at Fort Benning, Georgia. As soon as he was discharged, he applied for the police academy and was immediately accepted. Upon graduation, he returned to his home town in Kansas as half of the local police force, but found most of the work there boring. Then he applied for a job with the Denver police department and was accepted. He spent most of his career there, but only attained the rank of detective sergeant. We called him Joe Friday. He was married twice, but both marriages failed. He had a daughter by his first wife, but only had minimal contact with her. By the time we started the trip, he was still working out to stay in shape, but he seemed to lack purpose for his life.

My Uncle Mac was actually Walter McRae. He was my mother's older brother. Our family had been in Illinois for as long as anyone could remember. Any connection with Ireland or Scotland was long forgotten. Uncle Mac joined the Air Force after high school and became a navigator on C-130s, which had required a reserve commission. After spending four years hauling troops and equipment all over the world, he opted for the police academy. He graduated at the top of his class and used that distinction to secure a position on the Chicago police force. I never knew him very well as I was growing up. He would show up at family functions, each time with a different girlfriend, but he never married any of them during his working years. He was always somewhat of an enigma to me. He was my only uncle, and occasionally he would remember my birthday, but he remained rather detached. My mother idolized him as her big brother, the cop, but I hardly knew him back then.

I was greatly surprised when Uncle Mac showed up without a girlfriend for my graduation from Northwestern University, but he was friendly and showed an interest in my plans. It was as if he had suddenly recognized me as an adult worthy of his attention. When I told him that I had been hired for a position as a high school English teacher, but wouldn't start until August, he posed the big question.

As I already mentioned, he asked me if I would be interested in serving as the "designated driver" on a month-long trip to Alaska. We would be back long before my new job started. He went on to describe his police academy reunion and how he and three of his newly retired cronies planned to rent a fairly large Winnebago RV and set out in June, which was less than a month away. Details were still being developed, but "D-Day" was to be the 6th of June, which made sense to anyone with even the slightest knowledge of history. They planned to meet at the Minneapolis airport, where he would pick up the others, and set out from there. It would take close to a week of hard driving each way, which would leave about two weeks to tour Alaska and do some serious fishing. He was vague about how they would pay for everything, but he assured me that it would cost me nothing. My services as the principal driver would be my contribution. It sounded to me like too good a deal to pass up, and so I agreed. Actually, I welcomed the opportunity to get to know him better, since he had just breezed in and out of my life up to then.

During the next three weeks I researched the trip as best I could. In order to get to Alaska, we would have to cross the Canadian provinces of Manitoba, Saskatchewan, Alberta, British Columbia, and Yukon Territory. The last fifteen hundred miles, from Dawson Creek, B.C., to Fairbanks, Alaska, would be on the Alaska Highway, once known as the Al-Can. Soon it would be daylight for well over sixteen hours, which meant that we would never have to drive in the dark. We could expect a lot of rain, especially as we approached the Pacific coast. The total one-way distance was over four thousand miles. At least we wouldn't have to worry about heavy traffic. There were few cities after

Winnipeg. The more I studied the route, the more I realized that this was much more than a trip. It was an adventure. I felt a little apprehensive, but that was more than offset by an aura of excitement.

As I relate some of the conversations which took place during the trip, I have decided not to try to duplicate the speech patterns of the four subjects. I took notes, but I did not use a recording device. Furthermore, the trip took place well over twenty years ago. I have also taken the liberty of "expurgating" some of the faulty grammar and obscenities. Therefore, my accounts of their remarks reflect my recollection of what was said, but not exactly how it was said. That is why the dialog will tend to appear somewhat the same, as if their remarks had been expressed by me.

2

On the morning of June 6, 1985, I flew from O'Hare airport in Chicago to Minneapolis, where my Uncle Mac met me. He had flown there two days earlier to rent the RV and make some other preparations. I was the first to arrive. It was almost noon before Bill Roberts arrived from Denver. Mac drove the Winnebago around to the door outside the baggage claim area, and we all got in. They all knew who I was and why I was coming along, but I could see that it would be a while before I was totally accepted. Each of them all had at least thirty years and a world of experience on me. I couldn't do much about that.

Uncle Mac drove as we left the airport. Although I was accustomed to driving in the heavy Chicago traffic, I wasn't used to driving a big RV. It occurred to me that even though I'd done a lot of city driving, they had all logged thousands of miles in the line of duty. I was easily the least experienced driver in the group. Realistically, I was just there because I preferred Pepsi to Budweiser.

Mac drove us to Interstate 94 and stopped at the first rest stop. He had picked up some ham and cheese sandwiches, which took care of lunch. He said that we would only go as far as Fargo, North Dakota, where we would spend the night and buy some groceries and beverages. The next day we would be in Canada.

Mac continued to drive all the way to Fargo. He didn't

want me to start driving until the traffic was lighter. At Fargo we stopped at a grocery store to pick up a few items, then drove to a KOA camp site to spend the night and take a shower. We agreed then not to shave during the rest of the trip, mainly as a practical matter, but partly as a macho lark. There we got a crash course on the functioning of the Winnebago, which would be our home for the next month. A tank of propane fueled the stove and the heater. There was a small refrigerator, but since it was mostly filled with beer, there was little room left for perishable food. We would probably have to buy ice along the way for anything else. There was a toilet and a shower, but the capacities of both would be strained if we used them very much. It was decided that the shower stall was to become an extra storage space. We would have to refill the water tank and drain the waste water tank frequently. Sleeping accommodations were tight, but adequate for the five of us. Shades on the windows could be lowered, since periods of darkness would be shorter as we drove northward. We all turned in early in anticipation of the next day.

❖

We arose at dawn the next morning and ate a quick breakfast at a fast food place. Then we headed north toward the border. As we followed the Red River, one of the group, I forget which one, commented, "This is an unusual river. It flows northward until it empties into Lake Winnipeg, and from there on to Hudson Bay. But because it flows slowly northward, it runs into ice in the spring. If there's a lot of snow melt, it floods. The Canadians built a by-pass around

Winnipeg, but some of the others, like Fargo-Moorhead and Grand Forks, aren't so lucky. They get flooded a lot."

Fortunately for us, it was June, so we didn't have to worry about that.

It was close to noon when we reached the Canadian border. Crossing into Canada was simpler then than it is now. We all knew that no firearms were allowed, a restriction which was somewhat difficult for four ex-cops who had been carrying handguns for the past twenty-five years. There was also a limit as to how much beer we could bring in. Uncle Mac knew that and had planned accordingly. They would have to buy Canadian beer until we reached Alaska. We cleared customs quickly and went to the currency exchange to get enough Canadian dollars to take us to Alaska. Credit cards were just coming into general use and hadn't become as international yet, so it was not surprising to see the four exchange cash. However, I was surprised to see how much cash they were carrying, especially Uncle Mac.

As we passed the first gas station, I was a little mystified by the listed prices. The rate was for Canadian dollars per imperial gallon, which was about five quarts. Canada hadn't gone entirely metric yet. I was glad that I wasn't paying for the gas. That way, I didn't have to figure out how much we were actually paying for it.

I took the wheel of the Winnebago shortly after we had cleared customs. Our next stop would be the outskirts of Winnipeg, where we planned to eat supper and look for a campground. There we would pick up Highway 1, the major cross-country highway. My four passengers sat at the table, drank beer, and engaged in a lively discussion. I found their conversations quite interesting and decided right then to keep a journal for my own information. I hardly suspected that I would be using it some twenty-five years later to reconstruct an account of their revelations.

When we reached Winnipeg, we turned west on Highway 1 and found a restaurant that seemed to satisfy everyone. As we were waiting for our food, Ben Randall commented, "The roads up here seem a lot better than the one I traveled farther to the east. I once drove from Thunder Bay, Minnesota, to Niagara Falls. It was over a thousand miles, and we were in Ontario the whole time. The road was mostly two-lane, and some of the bridges were one-way at a time. And that was a major east-west highway."

Uncle Mac commented, "That's because the country is a lot more rugged there. It's really rocky near the Great Lakes. We'll be crossing the prairie provinces for the next couple of days. It's easier to build good roads when you don't have to blast through rocks."

Karl Schultz added, "I've taken fly-in fishing trips to northern Ontario, and there were hardly any roads other than a few logging trails. Looking down from the plane, there was water everywhere. I don't see how they could build much of a road up there."

I decided to show off the results of my area study and said, "I read that Canada has more lakes than all the rest of the world combined. I find it remarkable that even though it's our 'neighbor to the north,' most Americans know very little about it. The Canadians follow our news and entertainment much more than we do theirs. The whole country has a smaller population than California, and it's heavily concentrated within a hundred miles of the U.S. border."

Bill Roberts shook his head and said, "It's hard to

imagine most of a great big country farther north than Minnesota. We call International Falls the ice box."

I picked up again, "Now try to imagine people living up above the Arctic Circle. Indigenous people have been living up there for centuries. The Inuits range all the way from northern Alaska to Greenland, and they manage to stay alive with practically no firewood and little vegetation. They learn to eat raw meat and fish because they have no way to cook it most of the time. They've avoided unwelcome incursions better than most native people, though, because hardly anyone else wants to live where they do."

Karl Schultz shuddered. "I get a chill just thinking about it," he said.

Eventually the topics of conversation changed to other subjects, but I sensed that I had gained a measure of acceptance just because I had taken the trouble to research where we were going.

❖

The next day we started our long drive across the prairie provinces: from Manitoba across Saskatchewan and Alberta. The highway was remarkably good, but the scenery was monotonous. It was green at that time of the year, but there were only ponds and small lakes inhabited by waterfowl to break up the long stretches of flat country, much of it cultivated with wheat fields. It reminded me of the American Midwest, only greener, wetter, and lacking corn fields.

For the first two days the conversation flowed easily, but eventually it began to slow down. The next large city was Regina, Saskatchewan. Someone mentioned that the Canadians pronounced it to rhyme with "vagina." I informed them that both words were originally Latin. "Regina" was "queen," and "vagina" was "scabbard." They found the etymology of the latter crudely amusing, but weren't particularly interested in how the Romans pronounced either of the two.

As we approached Regina, we saw a sign which indicated the distance to a town with the interesting name of Moose Jaw. That reminded Karl Schultz of a story which he felt compelled to share with us: "Two Canucks were driving this way when they saw the sign to Moose Jaw. The driver asked the passenger if he would like to go there. The passenger replied, 'Naw, there's nothing there but hockey players and whores.' The driver took offense and said, 'My wife is from Moose Jaw.' The other man thought fast and asked, 'Oh. What position did she play?'"

Not to be outdone, Uncle Mac related, "I once knew a man who moved up here. He didn't live very long, though. He saw a billboard that read 'Drink Canada Dry,' and he tried to do it."

The others laughed and took their turns telling raunchy jokes for about an hour.

3

At Regina we left Highway 1 and headed northwest toward Saskatoon. The highway was still good, but the weather deteriorated. It started raining. The combination of a dreary day and unimpressive scenery dampened the mood, and the lively conversation ended. Since nobody was anxious to cook when he didn't have to, we stopped at another restaurant in Saskatoon. There Karl Schultz was the first to express his frustration.

"I'll be glad when we get closer to the mountains," he said. "At least there should be something to look at."

"We need to find something to do besides looking out the window at nothing," Bill Roberts added. "We're still a long way from Dawson Creek. Too bad that none of us likes to play cards."

I had been mulling over an idea, but had been reluctant to mention it until then. However, this seemed like the time if there ever were to be one.

"Have any of you ever heard of Boccaccio's Decameron?" I asked with some trepidation.

Karl Schultz responded, much to my relief. "Sure. The Italians made a movie about it. I saw it in Heidelberg with a German sound track when we were back there visiting a few years ago. Some pretty raw stuff."

I seized the opportunity. "Some of it is, but it's about some people in a situation similar to ours. The bubonic plague swept Europe back in the fourteenth century, and supposedly ten people went to a villa in Italy to escape it. Since they had a lot of idle time to kill, like we do, they decided that each of them would tell a story on a given theme every day. That continued for ten days. So ten people, ten days, a hundred stories. That's the 'deca' in Decameron."

Karl shrugged. "The movie showed some priests and nuns doing some naughty stuff. How would we relate to that?"

I replied, "Yes, the book was banned by the Church for a long time because of the racier parts. But you could tell stories from your police experiences on an entirely different track. The similarity is just that you're confined and bored, as were the characters in the story, although in a different way."

Ben Randall spoke for the first time. "It sounds a little crazy to me, but it might be a way to kill time when we have nothing better to do."

Uncle Mac asked, "What kind of story would you have in mind for starters?"

I had been thinking about it and replied, "How about the most memorable person you ever served under? It could be positive or negative."

"Would it have to be a police supervisor?" Ben asked.

I shrugged. "I'd leave it wide open. Maybe it was someone in the military. You all had some of those."

The four were quiet for a while as they thought about it. Then Uncle Mac said, "I'm game. We can think about it tonight and try it tomorrow on the road."

The others agreed, if somewhat reluctantly.

That was the beginning of my indoctrination into some

unexpected revelations about my traveling companions—and maybe the darker side of police work.

❖

Here is the first round of stories about supervisors. I've condensed them quite a bit, but I've tried to recapture the essence of each.

> Ben Randall: When I was a rookie cop in Kansas City, I was quite a bit older than the others and more experienced, but I still had a lot to learn. The routine was vastly different from anything in my experience with the Nebraska state police. There was a sergeant named Wyatt who was a sort of mother hen to those of us who were new to the system. He gave us a lot of free advice, sometimes more than we wanted. I soon noticed that he was at work before any of the rest of us arrived and was still there when we went home. After a while I got the impression that he didn't have much of a life aside from his job. He stayed on until he was forced to retire at sixty, and then he still came in most days. I don't think he lived more than a year after he retired. It was only after he'd died that I found out he was married. When I met his wife at his funeral, I could see why he didn't like to go home. She was a shrill, negative woman who must have nagged him unmercifully. With a wife like that and no hobbies, the poor guy just buried himself in his work. With that gone, he had no reason to go on living.

Karl Schultz: For a short time I served under a sergeant who had a really bizarre sense of humor. He loved to play pranks on us. One of his favorite games was to pair us off with partners who really didn't do much to complement us other than our names. He matched a rookie named Martin with one named Lewis. He thought it was hilarious to pair Black with White, especially since Black was white and White was black. When women were accepted on the force, he delighted in assigning a male-female pair to an all-night stake-out. Since most people can't go that long without at least having to pee, the guys would always take along a jar or a bottle. With a mixed pair, that created a whole new set of problems. To their credit, they never told him how they resolved the issue, but they were probably the happiest when he was transferred to a different precinct.

Bill Roberts: For about five years I worked under a captain who was practically a legend. Maybe he had seen too many John Wayne movies, I don't know, but he had received three commendations for valor by the time I arrived. When there was a hostage situation, he would be the negotiator, sometimes walking in unarmed. When there was a shoot-out with hard-core types who had nothing to lose, he would be on the front line. He had killed more criminals than the state had executed. He was in his fifties when I met him, but he hadn't lost any of his aggressiveness. He still worked out daily and went to the pistol range every Thursday. The ACLU denounced him regularly as some kind of a Neanderthal, but he didn't care. He had his own epithet for the ACLU. But eventually the odds caught up with him. He was in the middle of a fire fight with a gang from a Mexican drug cartel when he took a bullet right in the stomach. I was there in his hospital room when he made his final pronouncement. It wasn't original, but I'll never forget it. He said, "You know, there are some old cops and some bold cops, but there aren't many old, bold cops." He had lost too much blood before he got to the hospital to survive. We lost a true hero that day.

My Uncle Mac spoke last: I'm going to be somewhat unconventional here. I've served under a lot of people: good, bad, and indifferent. Some were in the military, some in the police, some elsewhere. But the one I remember best was an elderly woman who hired me to mow her lawn and do some chores when I was sixteen. She had been a school teacher, had never married, and had inherited enough money to allow her to maintain a big house on a couple of acres. She was probably over eighty when she hired me. She was always pleasant without being overly friendly. One day I had finished mowing the lawn and went inside to collect my five dollars, which was pretty good pay back then. She was lying on a couch in her living room and apparently not feeling very well. She told me that her purse was on the table in the hallway. I was to pick up my five dollars and leave. I thought it rather strange, but I did as I had been told. When I opened her purse, I found a considerable amount of cash. The thought crossed my

> mind that I could take some of it, and she would never know the difference. But I dismissed the idea, took my five dollars, and left. She never mentioned the incident again, but I was always fairly sure that she knew exactly how much money was there. She didn't mention it because she didn't have to. I always wondered what she would have done if I had taken more than I should have. The lesson I learned from the experience is that if you do what you're supposed to, you don't have to worry about any negative consequences later on.

They added a few more impromptu stories, but those were the main ones on the subject. At least it got them to open up and reveal a little about themselves. With time, it would become more personal.

4

We crossed from Saskatchewan into Alberta, and it kept raining. I proposed that for the next Decameron topic we focus on the acceptance of women into the police forces. The four had plenty of time to think about the subject as we approached Edmonton. Because of a major oil discovery, a large city had been developed out in the middle of an empty prairie well north of Montana. It even boasted of having the largest shopping mall in the world. Since none of us was in a shopping mood, we passed on the mall and just looked for places to buy gas, beer, and food. We also needed to take on water and drain the sump. It took us a few hours to accomplish all of our objectives, and we continued in a northwesterly direction toward Dawson Creek in British Columbia. The rain let up shortly after that, and we were able to appreciate the sight of trees as we left the prairie and approached the foothills of the Rockies.

The improvement in the scenery was not enough to preclude our game, and so it continued. Here were their comments on female cops:

> Ben Randall: When I first became a cop, the only women connected with our work were clerical types, dispatchers, and meter maids. None of them carried firearms. The change came in the Seventies, about the same time the service academies went

co-ed. There was a lot of opposition from the old-timers, but it was going to happen. Of course, the standards had to be adjusted. Traditional cops had to be at least five-ten and physically fit, but few women are that tall and not likely to have played football. At about the same time, the entertainment industry decided to cash in on the new trend and showed female cops who looked like last year's prom queen. I never saw any who looked much like Angie Dickenson, though. They tended to be fairly large, plain-looking women. They knew that they had something to prove, and they set out to do just that. Some actually cringed when one of the others took maternity leave. I'd have to say that most of them tried hard to fit in and endured a lot of crude remarks along the way. It still grates on some men when a woman is promoted to a supervisory position, but that's just the way the system is moving. There's no going back to the old ways.

Karl Schultz: I agree with most of what Ben said. I'd go a step further with the entertainment comment, though. There was a TV series about two women who were supposed to be police partners, but they looked like they couldn't even have stopped someone from spitting on the sidewalk. We never put two women together except to investigate. It seemed to me that they were the most useful when they questioned female assault victims. Women who have been beaten or raped are more likely to talk about it to another woman than to a big lug like me. I was skeptical about the whole idea at first, but I've learned to appreciate them. But having said that, if I need someone to cover my backside in a tight situation, I want a partner with a pair of balls.

Bill Roberts: I'll go beyond that. I didn't believe in putting women in combat units in the military, and I don't want to see them facing down hardened criminals. Both situations are about the same. You can call me a dinosaur or a male chauvinist if you like, but I believe that women are the care-givers and men are the providers and protectors. Or at least they should be. If I get into a dangerous situation, I don't want to call for a woman to come to my rescue. I've seen women wounded in action, and it goes against my whole set of values.

Uncle Mac: He's right. It seems to me that the women's movement has progressed from women's suffrage to women's equal suffering. I believe in equal rights and equal pay for women. I like women, at least most of them. I've loved quite a few of them. I even had a female partner for a while. But I don't want to see them exposed to the kind of mayhem that I've experienced more than once. I'd hate to think that we don't have enough able-bodied men to deal with the scoff-laws and sociopaths out there without having to arm our wives, daughters, and sisters to go out and face them. I've seen both men and women with gunshot wounds. I can handle the former. I'm appalled by the latter.

A lively discussion ensued with no major disagreement.

5

Between Edmonton and Dawson Creek I suggested the next Decameron topic: When were you in the most dangerous situation and how did you handle it? While they were thinking about it, I used a rest stop to recite what I had researched about the Alaska Highway:

"Shortly after Pearl Harbor, the Japanese invaded Singapore, Hong Kong, the Philippines, and several more islands. One of these was Attu, at the far end of the Aleutians and technically part of Alaska. The U.S. responded by relocating Aleutian natives to mainland Alaska for their protection. The government also wanted to prepare for further Japanese attacks against Alaskan territory. At that time, there were no roads between Dawson Creek and Fairbanks except for some local roads in places like Whitehorse in the Yukon. It was decided that a joint U.S. and Canadian effort would be made to build a gravel road diagonally across the Rockies to connect Dawson Creek and Fairbanks. One team started at Dawson Creek and another at Whitehorse. It was a monumental task. Not only was the terrain rugged, it also contained swampy areas full of bloodthirsty mosquitoes. Sometimes the bulldozers broke through permafrost and sank into soft mud. But they persisted and completed the project in about two years: over fifteen hundred miles of road running diagonally across a mountain range. Today the road is paved, but it takes constant summer maintenance to keep it open. Somewhere along the line it was re-designated the Alaska Highway rather than the Al-Can. We won't make very good time on it. The speed limit is 50 mph or less for much of it."

Karl Schultz had a story to add to my narrative. He told us, "When I was in Ontario on a fishing trip, I heard about a segregated unit of black Army engineers that was working on the road way up north. They encountered some natives there who had never seen any outsiders. Supposedly, one of the natives told someone, 'This was the first time I ever saw a white man, and he was black.'"

❖

As we approached British Columbia, someone commented on how much longer the periods of daylight were becoming. In addition to our northerly advance, we were approaching the summer solstice, and soon it would hardly be dark at all. That meant that we could start as early as we wanted and drive until bedtime without ever driving in the dark. To compensate for my long days in the driver's seat, one of the others usually started behind the wheel and took the first shift in order to give me a break until they'd had a few beers. They were pretty careful about that after having cited so many drivers for DWI over the years. We also broke up the trip with frequent rest breaks. That helped relieve the strain on the toilet, as well as giving us a chance to stretch our legs.

After one such rest stop, we continued the Decameron game: What was your most dangerous situation and how did you deal with it?

Ben Randall: I don't know if I could pick just one. There were at least three times when my partner and I were called to break up a domestic dispute and found that someone had taken it to the next level. I remember one in particular where we found a man all distraught and threatening to kill his wife, himself, and anyone else who got in his way. When my partner tried to reason with him, the guy tried to shoot him. Luckily, he missed. I didn't wait for him to try again. I tried to wing him, but I was a little off target and hit something vital. He died in the ambulance. The guy had never gotten into trouble with the law before. Something just set him off, and he went berserk. I never killed anyone who really deserved it, but I killed a poor schmuck who just went off the deep end. I had trouble sleeping for a long time after that.

Karl Schultz: I didn't get into many fire fights. My worst spot came when two of us tried to arrest a man in a bar, and several of his friends objected. We found ourselves outnumbered five to two. Fortunately for us, we were sober, and they weren't. I broke three fingers on my right hand and had to use my left fist, but we finished what we'd come to do and left the others with something to think about. I didn't see any point in trying to press the finer points of the law. We caused some broken noses and extra income for a few dentists. I doubt if they ever tried to start a slug-fest with any cops again.

Bill Roberts: My scariest situation involved a car

chase. My partner and I were on a routine patrol in Denver when the dispatcher called us and told us that a highway patrolman had tried to pull somebody over, but the guy took off. The trooper backed off when the nut passed seventy in downtown Denver and was doing a slalom around the other cars. He was headed north on Interstate 25 and was still several miles inside the city limits. We spotted him with no problem. Everyone was honking at him. That's when I found out that my partner had been a stock car racer. Just as we got close to the guy, he pulled a fast u-turn across the median and headed back the other way. I was ready to let somebody else chase him, but I wasn't driving. We were doing close to eighty as we headed back to the center of town. People were taking the ditch to get out of the way, and I was trying not to lose my lunch. Finally we could see that a lane was closed ahead, and traffic was constricted. Our prize tried to maneuver around the left shoulder, but there wasn't enough room, and he had to stop. That's when we found out that we'd been chasing a seventeen-year-old kid. He got out of his car and grinned at us as if he'd just lost some kind of a game. When we asked him why he did it, he replied that he was afraid of what his mother would say if he got a ticket. I never found out what she said to him when she visited him in jail.

Uncle Mac: I was in several tight situations, but we usually had the advantage. But once there was a bad guy who nearly cancelled out our edge. We were making a drug bust on the south side of

> Chicago. A gang was holed up on the fourth floor of an apartment building. We had all the exits covered and seemed to have the situation under control. But when we broke into the apartment, one of the perps poured a gallon of gasoline on the floor and held up a cigarette lighter. He said he would rather burn and take some people with him than go back to prison. He ranted on for several minutes while our self-appointed negotiator tried to reason with him. I waited as long as I could, but the talk didn't seem to be going anywhere. So while he was looking the other way, I took careful aim and shot him in the head. We had to evacuate the building until the gasoline could be cleaned up, but nobody else got hurt. It could have ended a lot worse.

I thought that there would be a lot of discussion afterward, but there wasn't. It seemed that they were not accustomed to talking about such topics. It reminded me of what I had heard about combat veterans. Most were reluctant to talk about the most frightening events in their pasts. They relegated them to their nightmares.

6

We saw our first moose before we reached Dawson Creek. Someone commented, "We wouldn't want to hit one of those. They're as big as a horse."

Bill Roberts replied, "I've heard that they can do serious damage to the front of a semi. Just imagine what they could do to a small car."

Karl Schultz added, "I read about a woman in Alaska who hit one with a Volkswagen. She just knocked the legs out from under it, and the body crashed into her windshield. Then it kicked that little car to pieces. She was lucky to come out alive."

Ben Randall had the last word on the subject. "I've been told that they get on the railroad tracks in the winter to avoid the deep snow. Up here a locomotive's cow catcher is called a moose catcher."

Watching for wildlife became a prime source of entertainment, although we didn't see as many animals as we had expected.

❖

We rolled into Dawson Creek and found that it was dependent on tourists for much of its income. The parking lot of the small mall appeared to be the main gathering point as travelers stocked up for the long trip across the mountains.

We joined the rest and bought more groceries and Molson beer. As we observed the throng of fellow travelers, I could see that most of them were older people. That made sense, since the trip up and back could easily take two weeks. Working people with only two or three weeks of paid vacation would hardly want to spend so much of it just driving. There were entire caravans of retired people towing Airstream trailers. They tended to drive fairly short distances each day and camp at predetermined sites. Some spent all summer doing that, since they had no pressing need to return home.

Before we left, I pulled out a publication entitled Mileposts, which I had bought from the AAA branch office when I picked up my map. It gave considerable information about what we could expect to encounter on the Alaska Highway. We made good use of it from Dawson Creek to Fairbanks, and later on the return trip. The title of the publication referred to the markers which had been positioned the entire length of the highway. A tall post in Dawson Creek was labeled Mile "0."

As we left Dawson Creek on the two-lane highway, Uncle Mac asked me for the next assignment for our Decameron game. I had been thinking about it and replied, "How about the one that got away? The one you wanted to see in prison, but didn't."

Mac shrugged. "That shouldn't be too hard," he said. "I'm sure we all had some of those."

The two-lane highway was reasonably good for the first stretch. It continued through a heavily wooded area on fairly level terrain, but that soon gave way to a foretaste of the mountains. Much of the road had practically no shoulders, and the bushes grew right up to the road. Mac commented,

"I can see why the speed limit is so low. If you'd run off the road, you might disappear into the bushes, and nobody would be able to see you."

Ben Randall added, "Staying awake at the wheel shouldn't be a problem. This road wouldn't lull anybody to sleep."

At that point I felt compelled to give a geography lesson. "From here to Whitehorse we'll be going roughly parallel to the mountain range. They obviously built the road here because it was the easiest way to go—which doesn't say much for other possibilities. There are no roads to the coast from here until we're in the Yukon—maybe six hundred miles. Juneau is the capital of Alaska, but there are no roads to it because of the Coastal Range. The same for Petersburg, Ketchikan, and the other towns on the coast of the panhandle. You can only reach them by boat or pontoon plane."

Bill Roberts shook his head and said, "It must be like living on an island. What do people do there?"

I replied, "Natives have lived there for centuries. They survived mainly on fish and sea mammals, mostly seals but sometimes whales. More recently, other people moved there to build salmon canneries. Seasonal workers come up here in the summer just to work in the canneries or on commercial fishing boats. Some of my classmates at Northwestern came up to work one summer."

Karl Schultz added, "Tourism has also added to the economy. Cruise ships and ferries run from Seattle to southern Alaska up the coastal waterway. It's about eight hundred miles from Seattle to Haines, the closest connecting port. The cruise lines promote views of the glaciers and the wildlife, especially whales. It's a big business."

I was surprised that he knew that, but I didn't say anything. Apparently I wasn't the only one who had researched the trip.

A short distance out of Dawson Creek, we crossed the surprisingly wide Peace River. Once again I marveled at the engineering ability of the men who had built a bridge to span such a torrent. The river looked anything but peaceful.

We stopped for the night at one of the many gravel pits which had been dug to provide material for the constant road maintenance. It took us a while to get to sleep, since even with the blinds drawn, it still wasn't very dark.

The next morning I fried bacon and eggs for breakfast, and we started out with Uncle Mac driving the first leg. The scenery was rather monotonous, and so the four decided to continue their story telling. The theme was "the one that got away."

> Uncle Mac: Being from Chicago, our most spectacular failure was in not solving the disappearance of Jimmy Hoffa, the union boss. A lot of people turn up missing every year, but most of them are rebellious teen-agers or other people who just don't want to be found. Sometimes we never find out why someone has disappeared and, in most cases, don't try very hard to find them. We have limited resources. But in the Jimmy Hoffa case, it was obvious that someone had helped him disappear. Since he was a high-profile figure, we were instructed to follow every lead, investigate every tip, drag lakes, and dig up fields. But we never did find anything. Some people theorized that Martians had abducted him, but we were pretty sure that it was just some Earthling who had a special reason to have him removed. We had our

range of theories, but none of them panned out. When all was said and done, it seems that someone got away with murder.

Ben Randall: I never dealt with any celebrities, so I can't compete with that story. But I can think of several cases that we never solved. I wasn't a detective, but I did my share of pick-and-shovel work to aid in the effort. A few years ago there was a string of burglaries in a higher-class residential area in northern Kansas City. It appeared to be the work of one individual. He always struck during the day, when the occupants were at work or otherwise out of the house. We checked meter readers, delivery men, letter carriers, anyone who appeared to have a legitimate reason to be there, but we came up empty. Eventually it stopped. We can only guess why. Maybe he didn't want to press his luck. Maybe he moved away. Maybe he got hit by a truck. We just don't know. We never caught him.

Bill Roberts: About ten years ago we had an incident where an insurance executive was shot and killed in his car as he waited at a traffic light. I was one of the detectives assigned to the case. A witness actually saw it happen and got part of the license plate number, but the plate turned out to be stolen. We interviewed a lot of people who knew the victim and found out that he wasn't very popular, but the only person who seemed to have any good reason to kill him was his wife. They had no children, so she was his sole beneficiary. His life insurance policy alone was worth about a million. However, the wife was out of town visiting her sister when the incident occurred. That still left the possibility that she might have had an accomplice—either a boyfriend or a hired gun. But even though we were about ninety-nine percent sure that she was somehow involved, we couldn't prove it. She sold all of their property, collected the life insurance money, and moved to Hawaii. Who said that crime doesn't pay? Sometimes it pays big-time.

Karl Schultz: Shortly after I'd moved back to Milwaukee, I helped catch a small gang of drug dealers who were selling to college kids. The leader of the pack was a foreign student from Venezuela. But shortly after we'd made the arrest, the guy's father showed up at our precinct. He showed his credentials as a member of the Venezuelan consulate in Chicago and claimed diplomatic immunity for his son. We had to get a ruling from the State Department, but they told us that the claim was legitimate. We couldn't try the punk, but we could have him deported as an undesirable alien. I had the privilege of escorting him to O'Hare airport in Chicago and seeing him off. He grinned and waved at us as we let him go. But there's a postscript to the story for those who like happy endings. We learned that he got involved with the wrong crowd back home and paid the full price. So in a sense, we got him the death penalty. We didn't send his family a sympathy card.

The four had several more such stories to tell as we made our way to the Yukon.

7

For the next two days we drove through a part of the world which had hardly been touched by civilization. Most towns on the map turned out to be little more than gas stations. It was hard to imagine anyone wanting to live up there. The landscape varied from extremely rugged to flat and swampy. The trees tended to be smaller the farther north we went. The lakes were pristine and quite beautiful with eagles circling overhead looking for fish. The higher mountains were never far away, but not as close as they appeared to be. We would be driving somewhat parallel to the range as far as the Yukon, then angle westward and cross it at a more accessible site.

I found that my four companions knew little about the Klondike gold rush, which had started at the end of the nineteenth century, roughly half a century after the California gold rush. I tried to summarize it for them out of my scant research. I told them that thousands of people from all over the world had flocked to the Yukon in the hope of striking it rich. Gold always seems to have that kind of allure for people, especially those who have little else going for them. A small fraction of them found what they were looking for but, predictably, the majority did not. After a few years, most of the readily accessible gold had already been found, and mining was left to the big companies. Most of the prospectors had little reason to stay, but some did. The town of Whitehorse underwent considerable development during the rush and became the capital of Yukon Territory, all of which had just a few thousand inhabitants, including the native people. It reminded me of the saying, "This may not be the end of the world, but you can see it from here."

We bought gas at Fort Nelson, B.C., and Watson Lake, which was just across the Yukon border. We were still nearly a day's drive away from Whitehorse, so we stopped at the latter long enough to get a decent meal and tend to the Winnebago's needs. By then we were starting to wonder if there was any end to Canada.

As we approached Whitehorse, I made the suggestion that we take in the summer variety show. I had read in the Mileposts publication that every summer some theatrical college students go there and combine with the locals and a few professionals to put on a "Klondike Days" revue with lots of music and humorous skits. It seemed like it might be a good way to break up the last phase of the trip.

Whitehorse was a picturesque town of just a few thousand inhabitants. During the summer, there were often more tourists than locals there. Even as small as it was, it housed a substantial portion of the population of the Yukon. We arrived in mid-afternoon, just in time to get the last available tickets for the show. We found a place to park the Winnebago, restocked our supplies, ate supper, and made our way to the performance. The theater looked like something out of a western movie. It only had room for a small audience, which was just enough to accommodate the revolving number of tourists. The show turned out to be a semi-professional revue called "The Frantic Follies." Just as Mileposts had indicated, it was performed by a mixture of amateurs and professionals, but it wasn't at all obvious to us which were which. It was funny, musical, and very entertaining. The highlight was a dramatization of Robert Service's "The Cremation of Sam McGee." Robert Service was an Englishman who traveled the world and left his mark on the Yukon. Along with "The Shooting of Dan McGrew," his poem about Sam McGee is the best remembered. The skit ended with poor Sam sitting in the crematorium exclaiming, "It's the first time I've been warm." Even people who knew nothing about the poem or the Yukon applauded enthusiastically. It was a perfect way to break up a long trip. All of my traveling companions seemed pleased that we had attended the show.

❖

The next day we were in for a spectacle of a different sort. We drove close enough to Mount Logan to get an appreciative view. It is the highest mountain in Canada, over 19,000 feet high, and only a short distance from the Pacific Ocean. Mount McKinley is slightly higher, but it is also more remote. Without taking a plane ride, one can seldom see it because of the persistent cloud cover. But Mount Logan juts up like a massive cone within easy view from the highway. We were told that the venturesome people who have climbed it report that there is nothing visible living on top of it. It is too cold to support just about any form of life. None of us felt inclined to check out the accuracy of the observation. We just stood there with our mouths hanging open as we gazed at the enormous peak. It was one of those sights which one never forgets.

❖

From there it was a relatively easy drive to Fairbanks. We crossed into Alaska with no problem at the border. Shortly after that, we passed under the new trans-Alaska oil pipeline, which extended over six hundred miles from the north slope to the port of Valdez. Someone commented that the construction of the pipeline was an engineering feat which ranked right up there with the building of the Alaska Highway. As we approached Fairbanks, we drove through a town named North Pole. We speculated that they probably got a lot of mail addressed to Santa in December. An Air Force base was the last major site before we reached Fairbanks. Uncle Mac said that he had flown into there twice while navigating C-130s. The weather was sunny and surprisingly warm when we arrived at our northernmost destination. Since Fairbanks and Anchorage were the only two Alaskan cities of any size, we decided to drive around and look at it. One aspect that we noticed right away was that all the parking lots were equipped with jacks for plugging in head-bolt heaters. The reason became obvious when we visited a gift shop and bought post cards depicting a bank whose thermometer reading was minus fifty-nine degrees. We all bought cards to send back to our families and friends to prove that we had reached the extreme point of our trip. Another set of items in the gift shop amused us so much that we all had to buy some. Someone had come up with the idea of shellacking moose droppings and fashioning them into jewelry. We all bought earrings and necklaces made from moose turds. Even if we didn't know what we would do with them, we had to buy some. We thought it was hilarious. That probably says something about our sense of humor. A few years later I gave my future wife a set of the earrings. She was less amused than I had hoped and never wore them, as far as I know.

We drove by the University of Alaska and toured a native museum, which we all found interesting. Someone told us that we were a week too early to watch the traditional baseball game starting at midnight on 21 June, the summer solstice. The game required no lights, because by then it never got dark. We were also advised to take advantage of an outdoor supper featuring some of the Alaskan delicacies, salmon and halibut with wild blueberry cobbler for dessert. We decided right then to forgo chicken, beef, and pork and dine on seafood for the rest of the time we were in Alaska.

Leaving Fairbanks, there were not many options with regard to route. Aside from dead-end roads leading northward, the only way to go was south toward Anchorage. The Alaskan road net consisted of a loop with Fairbanks at the top and Anchorage at the bottom plus a few spurs leading outward, but ultimately going no farther. The vast majority of the state had no connected roads to speak of.

8

After Fairbanks, our next destination was Denali Park. I have to confess that up to then, I had never heard of this national park, which is larger than the state of Massachusetts. Aside from being the home of the elusive Mount McKinley, it was best known as a game preserve. Since the fauna included grizzly bears, the park was not open to hiking or camping. In addition to the bear danger, there was a problem with the water. It seemed that the moose had infested it with parasites in some places. Vehicles were allowed, but they had to be registered. The main form of transportation consisted of a fleet of yellow school buses. There was no charge for the tours, but it was necessary to register and specify how long a trip was requested. We agreed on a four-hour trip.

After waiting for an hour or two, we boarded a bus and headed westward. The terrain consisted mainly of rolling hills without many trees. We drove for half an hour without seeing any animals, but suddenly the driver stopped and pointed to a ravine. We raised our binoculars and looked to where he was pointing. It was a caribou. When some of the other visitors tried to get a long-range photo, it occurred to me that no one in our group had shown much interest in photography. Mount Logan had inspired some of us to dig out our cameras, but there appeared to be no shutter-bugs among us. None of us had ever seen a caribou, but we were all hoping to see a grizzly bear. Caribou weren't all that different from deer in appearance, except that both sexes grew antlers.

Our next sighting wasn't any kind of a wild animal. It was a hiker. Someone had defied the rules and set out across the hills on foot. His large backpack suggested that he intended to hike for some distance. The driver immediately radioed his dispatcher and told her about the hiker. After he had completed his report, our driver told us that the venturesome intruder would be unceremoniously escorted out of the park and might not even be allowed to retrieve his vehicle. The reason: Grizzly bears have been known to run down full-grown elk. An unarmed human would be likely to find out that he is not exempt from the food chain, particularly if he were to disturb a "sow" with cubs.

Soon after that, we found out that the driver was not just being an alarmist. About four hundred yards to our right we saw a sow with three cubs. They seemed to be accustomed to seeing the yellow buses and didn't pay much attention to us. We were surprised to notice how light their fur was. They were almost blond. We watched them for about twenty minutes before continuing our tour.

We saw a few more caribou and a moose, but no more bears. At the far end of the tour, we all got out for a rest stop at an appropriate facility. From there, the driver pointed to the southwest and told us that Mount McKinley was over there in the distance, but we couldn't see it because of the usual cloud cover. The natives called it Denali, which had carried over to the name of the park. It meant "the high one" in the Athabascan language. That seemed entirely fitting.

As we were heading back, a bird that resembled a grouse ran across the road. The driver told us that it was a ptarmigan and that it was the state bird. We made a mental note of it in case we should see any more. He also told about the annual migration of the caribou, when herds numbering over a thousand traveled great distances for better grazing. Many were lost every spring while trying to cross swollen rivers. It struck me that this was Alaska's version of the African wildlife migration, although on a somewhat smaller scale.

We saw a small herd of caribou on the return trip, but no more other large animals. Still, we felt more than satisfied with what we had seen. It had been an interesting trip, and it hadn't cost us anything. The next day we would be in Anchorage and back to semi-reality.

❖

One of the realities was that we needed to have the Winnebago serviced. We had driven about five thousand miles by then and still had a lot of tough driving ahead of us. When we reached Anchorage, we had no trouble finding a station that serviced RVs, since there were probably more of them in Alaska than anywhere else. While we were waiting for our home on wheels, we walked to a restaurant and ordered their specialty—king crab. It was one of the many delicacies which the coastal waters of Alaska offered. Our eating schedule had become rather capricious. We ate breakfast when we woke up, but with little exercise and constant daylight, we usually ate only one more meal the rest of the day, and it followed no pattern. We simply followed the beckoning of our stomachs.

After we had eaten and recovered our "mobile home," we drove around the city. It was fairly modern, but not especially impressive to the five of us, who all had lived in larger cities. The construction of the Alaskan pipe line had brought an influx of people looking for well-paying jobs. Some had stayed in Alaska; others had gone back home. But Alaska was no longer the least populated state. Wyoming could now claim that distinction.

We went to a grocery store to restock our modest supply of food and immediately noticed the high prices of fresh produce. We soon learned that Alaska had to import most of its fruit and vegetables, which came as no surprise. But we were surprised to learn that southern Alaska actually had a respectable growing season. We had already noticed a large number of private greenhouses and assumed that the growing season up here was too short for serious gardening. However, we learned that during the period of long daylight, some vegetables did very well. Cabbage and other vegetables which can endure a little frost did particularly well and grew to impressive sizes. Citrus fruits of course, were out of the question, as were many other standard crops of the lower forty-eight. My companions were careful about what they bought. I was just glad that I didn't have to pay for any of it.

We spent the night (or what passed for night) at a campsite on the edge of Anchorage, where we were able to shower and enjoy a few amenities. We weren't ready to shave, though, even if we were looking pretty scruffy. We were surprised when the camp supervisor warned us not to leave anything outside the RV. He told us that the immigrant job seekers had also included some opportunists who came around at night to see what had been left unattended. When I told him that we had four retired cops in our group, he just grinned. But we didn't leave anything outside just in case.

After we had settled down for the so-called night, one of the four asked me if I knew anything about the history of

Alaska. Once again, I was surprised to find so much intellectual curiosity among men who had not studied beyond high school, but I did my best to answer the question.

I attempted to summarize what I knew about the human development of Alaska in an abbreviated form. A few years later, James Michener would write one of his encyclopedic novels on the subject, but obviously that wasn't available yet. I told them about the presumed migration from Siberia across the later-to-be-named Bering Strait toward the end of the last Ice Age, some 14,000 years ago. Within a few centuries, humans had wandered to nearly every corner of the North and South American continents. However, some chose to stay in the far north. They would become the Inuits, the Aleuts, and several other groups. Nobody knows, after all this time, what their Asian languages were or just how they developed into separate linguistic groupings. In any event, those who chose to remain in the far North learned how to survive in the harsh environment. They caught fish in the rivers and bays, hunted sea mammals, and made their clothing from animal hides and furs. They must have dedicated their entire short lives to little more that survival. The idea of becoming vegetarians or vegans would never have occurred to them, because it would have meant almost immediate starvation.

The first Europeans to reach Alaska, as far as we know, were the Russians. They first arrived some two-and-a-half centuries ago, around 1740. They were quick to realize the value of Alaskan furs, particularly sea otters and seals. They eventually established their capital at Sitka, on an island. They introduced the Russian Orthodox Church, but forced the newly converted natives to hunt sea otters for them. Their policy toward the Aleutian natives was not unlike that of the Spaniards in Latin America. They considered the indigenous people human enough to become Christians, but beastlike enough to be treated as slaves. They were so successful in their pursuit of furs that they nearly annihilated the sea otter population. But by then the Russians were experiencing constant rivalry with other powers, primarily the U.S. and Great Britain. That, combined with the fact that they had little use for the inland territory, caused them to agree to sell their claim to the U.S. right after the American Civil War. Even though we got it for a bargain price, roughly two cents an acre, a lot of people objected. They called it "Seward's folly" and "Seward's ice box" after the Secretary of State, William Henry Seward, who had brokered the deal.

Gradually, people came to realize that it wasn't such a bad deal after all. There was a large variety of mineral resources, most notably gold and oil, and the waters off the coast were rich in sea food and aquatic mammals. But like northern Canada, much of it was inaccessible by land and impractical for development. It has been a state since 1959, along with Hawaii, but its remoteness is still considered a drawback by many people.

Karl Schultz spoke up. "I remember a story about a man who wasn't put off by the remoteness or the climate."

Bill Roberts rolled his eyes and said, "Here we go again!"

Karl ignored him. "It seems that right after Alaska became a state, there was a Texan whose pride wouldn't tolerate his living in the second-largest state. So he packed up and moved to Alaska. I don't remember just where he went, but he found an old-fashioned saloon and went inside. Four trappers were sitting at a table playing poker. The Texan strode over to them and announced, 'Well, here I am!' The trappers just looked at each other. The Texan continued undeterred, 'I want to become an Alaskan, since it's the biggest state now.' One of the trappers responded slowly, 'You know that in order to become a true Alaskan, you have to pass three tests.' The Texan shrugged and said, 'I'm ready. What are they?' The trapper glanced at his cronies and said, 'First you have to chugalug a fifth of whiskey. Second, you have to kill a polar bear. Third, you have to have sex with an Eskimo woman.' The Texan never flinched. He said he was ready. One of the trappers ordered a fifth of cheap whiskey, and the Texan gulped it right down. 'That was easy enough,' he said as he staggered out the door. The trappers chuckled after the Texan had left and went back to their poker game. Two days later the Texan came back. He was all bloody, and his clothes were badly torn. As the trappers looked at him in disbelief, he asked, 'Now where's that Eskimo woman I'm supposed to kill?'"

Thus ended the history lesson, even if it wasn't exactly the way I had intended. The four asked for my proposal for their next Decameron topic, and I suggested, "My worst day as a cop." They would have ample time to think about it, since there was more activity and scenic driving ahead.

9

From Anchorage, our next destination was the Kenai Peninsula, which extends south of the city. The usual place of interest was Homer, at the far southwestern end of the peninsula. It advertised itself as the halibut capital of the world, a claim which few could dispute. We intended to go there, but first Uncle Mac wanted to take the road down the eastern side of the peninsula to Seward, a town named after the aforementioned Secretary of State who had been so instrumental in the purchase of Alaska. It was also a fishing port, but it offered a more diverse assortment of fish, including red snapper.

When Bill Roberts heard that, he exclaimed, "I can't believe that we can catch red snapper up here. When I was stationed at Fort Benning, we used to run down to Panama City, Florida, to catch red snapper and black grouper in the Gulf of Mexico. You wouldn't expect to find the same kind of fish at such extremes of water temperature."

Shortly after leaving Anchorage, we saw our next new animal variety—Dall sheep. Cars parked beside the road indicated that something was going on. We looked up at the cliffs above us and saw about eight of the wild creatures—sure-footed animals which maneuvered on the high rocks much like their cousins, the Bighorns. We watched them for several minutes, then drove on. Soon we reached the fork which determined whether we would go to the right toward Homer or to the left in the direction of Seward. We turned to the left, realizing that we would have to come all the way back to the fork in order to reach Homer. Even though the two towns were at opposite sides of the peninsula, there was no connecting road. A high, rocky ridge separated them.

The road was narrow and rugged. Soon we reached a road repair site where we would have to wait our turn to proceed. It seemed like a good time to continue our story telling. Each one was to relate his worst day as a cop.

> Bill Roberts started: I can think of quite a few bad days, but the one that sticks out in my mind was one when we were looking for a little girl of about six. She was the daughter of a fairly wealthy couple who lived in Aurora. She had been abducted from a playground near their home, and the kidnappers telephoned with a demand for ransom money. The parents were frantic, but they called us in despite a warning not to involve the police. One of our negotiators dealt with the abductors over the phone off and on for about three days while our whole team tried to follow leads and find her. The parents were ready to meet any demands to get their child back. But apparently the kidnappers lost their nerve and took off, leaving her tied up. By the time we found her, it was too late. I had what was probably the worst moment of my life untying a dead child. Our guys eventually caught up with the kidnappers, and they were sentenced to life in prison. But that was small compensation. I nearly quit the force after that episode. It really got to me.

It got to the rest of us as well. Nobody spoke for several minutes.

Traffic, such as it was, started moving again, and it was decided that we would wait until evening to continue with this line of story telling.

We proceeded slowly toward Seward and took in the marvelous scenery, with a rocky escarpment on our right and the sea to our left. We reached Seward by mid-afternoon. It was a picturesque fishing village with a breath-taking view of the bay. A large parking lot provided a temporary home for the occupants of more RVs than I had ever seen in one place. This was undoubtedly due to the shortage of hotels, motels, and inns in Alaska. Most visitors were there either to go fishing or to take a sight-seeing cruise. Since we counted ourselves among the former, we made reservations aboard a fishing boat for the next day. It was a bright, sunny day, and so we all went for a walk. It didn't take long to see everything that comprised Seward. Then we went down to the docks to watch the fishing boats return to port. Most came in with decent catches of red snapper and a few smaller halibut. There were ample stations set up on the pier for the fishermen to clean their catches. As the rejected fish parts were released, swarms of sea gulls as big as chickens swooped in to feast on the entrails and other superfluous parts. After that, we looked for a restaurant to satisfy our appetites for more sea food. We didn't have to look far. We promised ourselves that we would be grilling our own supper the next evening.

After returning to our Winnebago, the other three resumed their story telling.

Ben Randall: We were frequently called to check

out reports of domestic abuse. Some of them were repetitious. One of those involved a Puerto Rican couple with three kids. The ethnic part doesn't matter. Abusers come in all shades and sizes. I was called to the home twice. Once we arrested the guy. But after the third time the wife dialed 911, the DA got a restraining order on her husband. He violated it at least twice, but nothing much was done about it. Too bad. The next time he went over the top. He shot his wife, all three kids, and finally himself. I could never understand why anyone would do such a thing, but it happens. For a time I was haunted by the feeling that we should have done more to prevent it. It took quite a while before I could finally let it go. What's done is done. We can't go back and fix it. If we agonize over every human tragedy, we can't keep doing our jobs.

Karl Schultz: My worst day stretched into several. One spring night my partner and I were called to break up a noisy party. We got there at about eleven and could hear the ruckus from a block away. It was from a house in the low-rent district. Nobody could hear us knock on the door, so we just went in. There were a dozen or more young people there, probably all college kids. They had been drinking, and there was a distinct smell of pot in the air. When I asked who was in charge, someone pointed to one of the young men. I got his attention and told him that the neighbors were complaining about the noise. He muttered a profanity and indicated what the neighbors could do with themselves. I told him that he would have to control the party or we would arrest the lot of them for creating a disturbance. He became belligerent and told me that we were exceeding our authority—but not in just those words. I moved to cuff him, but he turned and took a punch at me. He was too drunk to be effective, and I ducked his punch and slapped his face hard enough to give him a bloody nose. Then I cuffed him and asked if anyone else would care to join him. They all got quiet. My partner and I decided that it wasn't worth the extra paperwork to arrest the kid, so we let him go with a warning.

Well, that wasn't the end of the story. It turned out that the kid's father was a big-shot lawyer with political ambitions. He filed a complaint of police harassment against me. I was suspended from duty until the whole mess could be sorted out. It seemed that no one would admit to seeing the kid take a punch at me. Even my partner had been looking the other way. Internal affairs grilled me about the use of excessive force. It looked as if I could lose my badge and everything that goes with it. But then one of the girls from the party found out what was going on and came forward to testify that she had seen the kid try to hit me. I was exonerated and even received my full pay for the time I was suspended. I don't know what would have happened if that girl hadn't cleared things up for me. I owe her big time, but I don't even know her name.

Uncle Mac: My worst day occurred several times with a similar scenario. Each time, I was called to

> the scene of a fatal traffic accident. Two involved drunk drivers. One was due to icy road conditions. One was in broad daylight when someone apparently fell asleep at the wheel. In all four cases, seat belts probably would have prevented tragedy. Air bags surely would have, but they were just becoming available, and most cars didn't have them yet. In all four accidents, someone died, and the others survived with horrible injuries. I've been called to many other accident sites, but it was seldom that anyone died. Those four were the awful exceptions. I wish that there were some way to impress upon beginning drivers what an awesome responsibility it is to get behind the wheel of a vehicle.

It took me a long time to get to sleep after hearing that latest round of stories. I almost regretted having suggested that topic.

❖

The next morning we ate breakfast, then walked down to the dock. Two of us carried ice chests containing our lunch and beverages. The boat was equipped to handle about a dozen fishermen. As we motored out into the bay, we were treated to an avian show. There were sea gulls, terns, and other sea birds everywhere. Soon we started seeing puffins, the so-called sea parrots. As we gained some distance from the shore, an occasional eagle came into sight. We also got our first look at sea otters, the animal which the Russians had prized so highly for their pelts. They were almost comical creatures. They would dive down to the sea bed and bring up a clam, then float on their backs while they broke the clam and devoured the insides. We were intrigued by the show which Mother Nature provided.

Eventually we reached our first fishing spot. We dropped heavy lines baited with cut fish or squid. Activity was fairly slow, but occasionally someone would bring up a small halibut, a Pacific cod, or a red snapper. We kept only the snappers and released everything else. By the end of our designated time, we had eight decent-sized red snappers. That would take care of our suppers until we could catch some big halibut.

After we had returned to port, we cleaned our fish at the designated place and made some gulls very happy with the discarded parts.

10

Our day-long drive to Homer turned out to be one of the most interesting of the entire trip. We made our way back to the junction in a slow but steady fashion and were spared the long delay for road repair. Then we headed southward again along the coast of Cook Inlet. As we passed several streams, we saw many anglers trying to catch the spawning red salmon. We regretted not having the proper tackle to join them. A few miles from the junction we saw a sign indicating a glacier to our left. We took a short side trip in order to check it out. The dirt road followed a stream which was just a run-off from the melting glacier. In the following years, it would retreat considerably. As we gazed at the massive sheet of ice, we could see that chunks of ice had broken off from it and were floating in the stream. Karl borrowed a dip net from someone and captured a few pieces of glacial ice for our ice chests. Someone speculated that our new ice might have been frozen thousands of years ago. Interesting thought!

Farther down the road we saw a sign indicating something called Clam Gulch. We were due for another stretch break, and so we took the exit there. As it turned out, Clam Gulch consisted of a long expanse of beach where the tide was the most extreme in the world. The water line retreated for hundreds of yards every day, exposing a beach of ultra-fine sand which was the home of razor clams. People went out with long, stove-pipe-shaped shovels to lock for spurts of water which indicated the presence of a clam. Somehow the creatures were able to move up and down in a narrow channel and thus avoid attempts to catch them. They also had very fragile shells, which the pursuers were careful not to break. Since we had neither the shovels nor the inclination to participate, we just watched. After that experience, clam chowder has never been the same to me.

A short distance from there we saw cars stopped to read a sign. We joined them to see what it said. The message was impressive. It stated that this spot marked the westernmost point of any highway in the western hemisphere. It seemed all the more significant when we looked across Cook Inlet and could see mountains far off to the west. Ben Randall consulted the map and said, "Nome is over there about a thousand miles away, but there's no road connecting it to the eastern part of the state."

Bill Roberts speculated, "Maybe there will be some day. Every winter there's a dog sled race called the Iditerod running from near Anchorage to Nome, way over on the west coast. If they can run dog sleds through there, they could probably build a road."

Uncle Mac speculated, "Maybe they could, but they'd have to justify the cost versus the benefits. Besides, dogs can run on a frozen river. That wouldn't be much of a place to build a road."

Karl Schultz concluded the discussion. "I saw a documentary on television about how the Soviets handle the problem. They wait until it's about fifty below zero and run truck convoys on the ice up Siberian rivers to re-supply folks who, for whatever reason, live up there. It's so cold that they never turn the truck engines off. If they did, they'd never get them started again. With that capability, they don't have to think about building roads up there."

Once again I was surprised at the awareness of these men who had never gone to college, but who possessed more intellectual curiosity than most of my college classmates. The four had started calling me "the professor" because I was generally better informed than they. But I realized that, while I had an educational advantage of a formal sort over them, they had practical experience of a very different type. By then I felt that I had achieved a degree of respect from them which I readily subordinated to mine for them.

❖

We reached Homer by late afternoon. It was not much more than a place to charter fishing boats, but it was the self-proclaimed halibut capital of the world, which appeared to be justified, even if the sign on the edge of town read "capitol." The waters of Cook Inlet were home to the flat, meaty fish which could run up to four hundred pounds. The flesh of these fish was so delicious and easily prepared that it probably would have tasted good boiled. In order to prevent over-fishing, a limit of two per fisherman had been established. Most people caught more than two, but the extras could be released. Unlike red snapper and grouper, halibut could survive being hauled up from the bottom and released. We were virtually assured ten halibut among the five of us. It was just a question of how big they would be and how we would deal with them.

We watched as the boats came in. There was a small industry in photographing each group of fishermen with their catches. The fish typically ranged from about fifteen pounds to a little over a hundred. None was anywhere near four hundred pounds, although photos proved that such monsters were out there. We were all excited as we contemplated the next day's adventure. We also had to consider the disposition of our catch. What would we do with even a hundred pounds of halibut?

That evening, Karl Schultz asked a thoughtful question: "I assume that Cook Inlet wasn't named for some ship's cook. The map also shows a Bering Sea and a Bering Strait, which you've already mentioned. They must have been named for somebody important. Do you know who they were?"

I replied, "Vitus Bering was a Danish navigator. As I told you earlier, the Russians were the first Europeans to reach Alaska, as far as we know. But they had little experience at sea compared to the other European countries. A lack of warm-water ports was always a problem for them. They therefore relied on a Scandinavian to lead the exploration of their Pacific Coast at the east end of Siberia. Bering led their voyages of discovery to Alaska, but died on a return trip.

"James Cook was an English sea captain who probably saw more of the world than anyone else in his day, other than some of his crew. There was a long-standing theory that the northern continents must have been balanced by an equal land mass in the southern hemisphere, which he proved to be false. His voyages took him to Australia, around New Zealand, and even close to Antarctica. He also explored the western coast of North America and reached this inlet. He died at the hands of some irate Hawaiian natives. Maybe they objected to his calling their home the Sandwich Islands." I couldn't resist ending on a frivolous note.

The next morning we ate a quick breakfast and headed for the dock. The boat we had chartered was rigged for six, but since there were only five of us, we assumed that we would be the only ones there. We were mistaken. A tall young woman showed up as the sixth member. She was a school teacher from Minnesota who had flown up to Alaska with a female colleague. They had rented a car and were occupying a tent on the beach. However, the other teacher had suffered sea sickness in the past and had chosen not to go out. As we left the dock, the teacher, whose name was Marla something, expressed concern about the price which was being charged for cleaning the fish. Uncle Mac graciously assured her that we would clean and fillet her fish, since there would be only two.

We cruised out for just over an hour, enjoying the appearance of many puffins, the colorful little birds that looked like sea parrots. Eventually we stopped and dropped our lines baited with squid. The first catch was a Pacific cod, a less tasty cousin of the Atlantic cod. The driver cut its head off and used it for bait, which surprised those of us who were accustomed to baiting hooks with worms or minnows. Before long we started catching halibut. They were not particularly scrappy compared to other fish, but their sheer weight required us to exert ourselves to haul them up from the bottom of the bay. The driver kept a small-caliber rifle handy for dispatching the bigger ones at the surface. It would be dangerous to have a big flat fish flopping around our legs. It disturbed me a little to have a ten-pounder thrown back as too small, but we followed the advice of our driver. After about four hours, we all had an agreeable limit of halibut ranging from about twenty to fifty pounds. Except for Marla. She had caught one that was over five feet long and ran close to a hundred pounds. We had offered to help her pull it up, but she insisted in doing it by herself. Our chagrin was exacerbated by the fact that we would have to clean it. Thanks, Uncle Mac!

When we returned to port, we had our pictures taken with our catch. Then we had to decide what to do with it. After filleting our ten fish plus Marla's two, we estimated that we had about a hundred fifty pounds of filleted fish. The freezer compartment of our refrigerator was still full of red snapper from Seward. It was Marla who offered a solution. She had been doing some investigating while we cleaned the fish. She had found a dealer there who was accustomed to dealing with such dilemmas. He could hold our catch in a freezer until we returned to the "lower forty-eight" and then ship it to us, or we could trade some of it for a lesser quantity of smoked salmon. Karl and Uncle Mac opted to have most of theirs shipped. The rest of us traded ours for smoked salmon. I don't remember what Marla did with hers.

11

It was cloudy the next morning as we set out to return to Anchorage. As we passed the fishermen on the streams, we resolved to find a place where we could catch spawning salmon. Uncle Mac reminded us of the unusual cycle of these fish. They hatched far up a river or stream and swam downstream to the ocean. Then, after a long period at sea, they somehow found their way back to that original river and swam upstream. There the females deposited their eggs, the males fertilized them, and then they all died, having completed their life cycle. That raised the obvious question of how the whole process had started. It was rather like the question about the chicken and the egg. It simply defied logical explanation.

The return trip held no surprises, since we had just covered that stretch of road two days previously. Uncle Mac suggested that we return to the same campground outside Anchorage, where we could take on fresh water and drain our waste water, take a shower, and even wash some clothes at their coin-operated facility. With cool temperatures and minimal physical exertion, we had worn the same clothing for longer than we should have without becoming too offensive, but having cleaned fish twice altered the equation. The sea gulls were starting to eye us.

❖

I think it was Ben Randall who raised the question about the next topic for our Decameron game. I suggested one which would take little contemplation, since they would already have formed their own personal opinions: How do you feel about the death penalty? Their expressions told me that their opinions had already been formed.

We arrived in Anchorage by early afternoon, bought some groceries and beverages, and headed for the campground. There the clerk again warned us not to leave anything outside the RV at night—night by then consisting of about three hours of semi-darkness. He said that the thieves were still active.

After attending to our various chores, we grilled a delicious meal of red snapper and halibut. We were saving the smoked salmon for the road, since it required no cooking. By then the four ex-cops had decided to take turns watching for drive-by thieves. But since we were still hours away from darkness, we resumed our Decameron exercise with the death penalty as the topic.

> Again Bill Roberts started: I think it's noteworthy that western Europe has abolished the death penalty, whereas in parts of Asia they still stone people for adultery and lop the heads off criminals as soon as they have been convicted of a crime. That's an enormous range of punishment. We seem to be caught somewhere in the middle. Our Supreme Court has imposed a moratorium on capital punishment but will probably leave it up to the individual states to decide. Some consider capital punishment to be cruel and unusual punishment. Others say it's only unusual if you seldom carry it out. I find

myself ambivalent about it. I just think that if we're going to do it, we should come to an agreement as to how it should be done and make it uniform.

Karl Schultz was next: I think it's appropriate in some cases. Some people don't deserve to live after what they've done. My biggest objection is that after someone receives the death sentence, it takes ten years to exhaust all the appeals. By then, all too often, the perp has evolved into someone else, found religion, and apparently become a law-abiding citizen. And to me the ultimate irony is that if someone on death row requires any medical attention, the taxpayers have to cover his medical and pharmaceutical bills while we wait to execute him. If that makes sense, I'm the tooth fairy.

Ben Randall: I have trouble with our history of false convictions. We have had prisoners released after new evidence has cleared them. Then the governor says we're sorry, and they give the guy some money as compensation. If we execute somebody and then find out that he was railroaded, what do we do? Tell his wife or his mother that we're sorry? It doesn't happen very often, but it happens, especially to poor slobs who can't afford fancy lawyers. It's been said that no rich man has ever been executed in our country. I'd be more in favor of capital punishment if we could just be sure that we were only executing hard-core criminals who had no possible legitimate defense.

My Uncle Mac had the last say: I agree with Ben up to a point, but I'd take it a step further. After any kind of a natural disaster—flood, earthquake, tornado, whatever—some of the first people on the scene are the looters. They don't care what other people have lost. They just find an opportunity to grab something with little risk involved. I think that looters should be shot on sight. That would save the taxpayers the expense of trying them and would rid the world of some scum. That applies to burglars as well. I have no use for burglars. They break into your home and take something which they can sell for a fraction of its value and, in the process, shatter your sense of security. Nobody sleeps well after having been burglarized. If the home owner doesn't shoot them and we catch them, I would have no problem with the death penalty. They don't deserve to live. I also think we're too lenient with juveniles. A teen-ager who shoots someone is treated separately from his slightly older accomplice, depending on where the court decides to draw the line. To me, if someone is old enough to commit a serious crime, he's old enough to face the consequences. I've dealt with some hard-core fifteen-year-olds, both male and female. I don't advocate capital punishment for fifteen-year-olds, but neither do I go along with erasing their juvenile records when they're supposedly adults. They should be tagged and watched until they can show that they're no longer a danger to society. All of this means that we spend far too much on the dregs of our populace. I wish there were an island where we could send all of

> these miscreants and let them victimize each other and leave the rest of us alone. So am I opposed to the death penalty? No way.

Mac's passionate outburst sparked a lively discussion which followed until someone noticed that it was actually getting dark. Each of the four took a turn watching an ice chest which they had left on a picnic table as bait, but no thief showed up.

12

By asking at a sporting goods store, we got the location of a salmon fishing camp within reasonable driving distance. It was on a medium-sized river whose name I have forgotten. The camp specialized in floating large rubber rafts down the river, stopping at prime fishing spots, and retrieving rafts and fishermen downstream. A guide, bait, and tackle were included in the package. Our guide turned out to be a man about my age from Wisconsin named Pete. Both Karl Schultz and my Uncle Mac had caught salmon and steelhead trout in Lake Michigan, but the rest of us were novices to the sport. As we set out in the swift current, I was glad to have a guide who had some experience. He took us about a mile downstream and pulled us up on an open beach. We would be fishing for king salmon using roe for bait. About an ounce of salmon eggs was wrapped in cheesecloth to hold it together. I wondered why that would work, since spawning salmon weren't supposed to eat anything, but apparently it did. Pete, our guide, showed us how to cast and warned us that some kings weighed over fifty pounds. "If you hook one of those, you'll think you've snagged a freight train," he said.

We fished for quite a while, but didn't hook anything that even approached fifty pounds. I hooked one and lost it. Karl and Uncle Mac showed their experience by catching one apiece in the twenty-pound range. They had to quit after making their catches, since the limit was only one fish per fisherman. The rest of us were disappointed, but there was no guarantee. At least, we had all caught snapper and halibut. Finally we boarded the raft again and floated down to our pick-up site, where a flat-bed truck was waiting for the raft and a Volkswagen bus was waiting for us. Uncle Mac and Karl filleted the two fish there and gave the roe to our guide, since we didn't have any use for it. We would have to buy more ice to keep our catch, but we resolved to eat it before it could spoil.

As we drove back to the camp, Pete gave us a quick lesson on the five kinds of Pacific salmon. He told us that the kings, or Chinooks, were not only the biggest, but also the best eating, along with the smaller red, or sockeye, salmon. It seemed that the redder the meat, the better the taste. Next were the pinks, or humpbacks, and the silvers, also called cohos. At the bottom of the list were the chum salmon. They were also called dog salmon, because mushers fed them to the sled dogs. So there are five kinds of Pacific salmon with at least ten different names. That was easily more than we wanted to know. We didn't even want to hear about the Atlantic salmon.

Arriving back in camp, we learned that the bus-sized RV next to ours had been rented by a party of affluent German businessmen who fished every morning and had a beer party the rest of the time. When Karl spoke to them in German, they invited us to join them. Most of them spoke some English, so we were able to communicate. They insisted that I forgo my Pepsi and drink beer with them. I reluctantly complied, and I was the only one who showed any adverse effects from it, since I had never drunk more than two beers before then. I was thankful that Uncle Mac drove us the next morning as we headed for Valdez.

❖

Valdez is the port of the Alaska pipe line. Tankers sail up Prince William Sound to fill up with crude oil from the north slope, some six hundred miles away. To get to Valdez, we had to negotiate a mountain pass, then drop steeply for several miles. It strained my imagination to envisage building a pipe line over such terrain, but it had been done.

Just before we made our approach to the pass, we stopped for gas at the last station before Valdez, but they had already sold the last of their supply. We didn't anticipate any problem, however, because we carried a spare five-gallon container on the back of the RV. We climbed the steep road to the top of the pass and noticed immediately how much colder it was up there. We were glad to be dropping to the relative warmth of a lower elevation. But about half-way between the pass and Valdez, we came upon an older couple in a small RV who had run out of gas. Uncle Mac estimated that we could spare about two gallons of our reserve and still have enough in case we ran out. The couple was grateful and offered to pay us, but Uncle Mac declined the offer. We followed them the rest of the way, and we reached Valdez with the gas gauge needle showing empty.

As we were approaching Valdez, I reminded the others about the devastating 1964 earthquake which had hit this area. It had caused a tsunami which raced up Prince William Sound, inundating everything in its path with a wall of water. It had damaged Valdez so badly that the inhabitants had actually relocated the town some distance away. The only factor which mitigated the death toll and destruction was that there were very few people living on Prince William Sound back then.

Our main reason for taking the side trip to Valdez was to see the glacier there. It was one of many which extended all the way to the sea. Cruise ships enticed tourists to view them, but those of us traveling by land were generally out of position to see these spectacular remnants of the Ice Age. We decided to take a sight-seeing cruise rather than fish again, mainly because we didn't know what we would do with any more fish.

There was nothing remarkable about the town of Valdez, but Prince William Sound was something else. Even from there we could see an inlet fringed with mountains dropping almost vertically into the sea. I wondered how that would compare with a Norwegian fjord, but I still haven't seen any of those, so I don't know. We booked a cruise for the next day and found a place to park our Winnebago. Then we went for a walk around the town to stretch our legs and work up an appetite for more grilled halibut and salmon.

❖

The next morning we ate our bacon and eggs and headed for the cruise boat. There were about thirty or forty passengers aboard. We were to sail down the sound and eat lunch on an island prior to returning. We talked to some of the other passengers and found out that nearly all of them were from the "lower forty-eight." Only one couple was from Anchorage.

As we headed out, the usual number of sea gulls accompanied us. Within a surprisingly short distance, we could see the glacier to our right, a broad white ribbon of ice. As it reached the sea, chunks of ice of various sizes broke off and floated away. The ice in the water looked pale blue. Soon we saw bald eagles perched upon the larger floating blocks. They didn't seem perturbed by our nearness. As the number of ice chunks increased, one of the crewmen took out a big net and retrieved some of the smaller ones. He told us that some of it would be melted to provide the purest drinking water in the world, since it had been frozen before there was any human activity. There had been nothing to pollute it.

After that, we started to see sea otters floating on their backs with their clams or crabs. I couldn't imagine anyone wanting to kill such delightful creatures just for their pelts, but I was probably still a bit naïve. There were also seals of varying sizes occupying the marker buoys.

By late morning we reached the small island where we would have lunch. From the dock we walked to a large wooden building near the center of the island. We sat on crude wooden benches and enjoyed another novel Alaskan delicacy—soup made with chunks of salmon floating in it. We found it quite delicious.

As we headed back to reality, I felt overwhelmed by the almost primeval beauty of this place. It seemed to be one of the last unspoiled spots on the planet, even if oil tankers passed by occasionally. Four years later I learned of the oil spill there by the Exxon Valdez, and I have to confess that I cried.

Returning to port, we were faced with the realization that we would have to begin our long trip back. We didn't even think of supper, since we had gorged on the unusual meal on the island. In anticipation of a lot of idle time, Ben made a suggestion: "We've been seeing quite a few native people up here, and I know that there are a lot more back where we live. I don't know much about them or even what to call them. Maybe we could share what we know about them." The others agreed. The next phase of our discussion would take a side trip into the world of the indigenous people of North America.

13

We waited until we had cleared the pass to start the next round of discussions. By then the sky was overcast, and we weren't quite so inclined to stare out the window unless we were driving. It seemed like an appropriate time to start the next round. The topic: the original Americans.

> Uncle Mac: I'll pass on this one. The Indians I've seen have tended to be a sorry lot, but I don't claim to know why. Maybe they've been screwed over. Maybe they've tried to hold on to a way of life that isn't practical anymore. I just don't know.

> Bill Roberts: Having lived in Colorado for many years, I knew that we had a significant Indian population. I've been to Mesa Verde twice and seen the remarkable structures there, which show that not all Indians lived in teepees. I've also been to the "Four Corners," where Colorado, Utah, New Mexico, and Arizona meet. There the Indians have shops where they sell their hand-made jewelry and other items to tourists. I've also encountered some in various other capacities, and they didn't seem much different from anybody else. I find it hard to reconcile my experiences with what I've seen in the movies. Maybe they've become domesticated.

> Karl Schultz was next: We have some Chippewa in Wisconsin. They always seem to have some gripe about fishing rights which I don't pretend to understand. Now they've gotten some kind of a monopoly for running gambling casinos. I don't see the connection. On the one hand, they want to preserve their old ways, and on the other they want to compete with the Mafia and Las Vegas to cash in on human stupidity. Maybe they're just trying to get even with the rest of us for giving them a raw deal in the past.

> Ben Randall: I haven't dealt with very many of them. I've probably seen more up here than I ever did before. I'm just curious about why we call them Indians. We call people from India that, too. What do they call themselves? And why do we have reservations? If they're American citizens, why do some of them have to live on reservations? I have to admit that I never thought very much about their situation before.

I drew a deep breath as I realized that, for at least once, my seemingly impractical liberal education might have some value. Looking back in the rear view mirror, I saw four pairs of eyes trained on me as I began: "The story starts nearly five centuries ago, when Europeans first had continuous contact with the native people here. The Vikings were probably here several centuries earlier, but they didn't stay. When Columbus and his crew arrived, they called the natives 'Indios,' not because they thought that they had reached India, but because they had reached the West Indies. So what did the natives call themselves? We find that many of them just called themselves 'the people' in whatever language they spoke. It has become a recent problem to try to find an acceptable name for them. Canadians call them 'First Nation.' We call them 'Native Americans,' as a more recent substitute for 'Indians.' But there doesn't seem to be any single name that is acceptable to everyone.

"A curious sidelight to that is that for a long time we've been giving our athletic teams Indian names, often just 'the Indians.' Now there is some objection to such designation. Oddly enough, most of it doesn't come from the Indians, but from other people who think that the Indians might be offended. It's a mixed bag. Florida State University calls its teams the Seminoles, but they have the approval of the Seminole council. The University of North Dakota calls its teams 'the Fighting Sioux.' They have two problems. First, there are too many branches of Sioux to get much of a consensus from them one way or the other, and secondly, they prefer to be called Lakota. 'Sioux' was an Ojibway derogatory term for the enemy. The easiest solution for a lot of schools appears to be just to drop the Indian names altogether. It seems a little peculiar that nobody fusses about the Fighting Irish or the Vikings, but some get upset about using an Indian name.

"Anyway, back to history. The reaction of the first Europeans was similar to that of those who encountered indigenous people elsewhere: in Africa, Australia, New Zealand, Hawaii, other Pacific islands, wherever. The assessment was that these were not fully human beings. It isn't hard to understand why the newcomers thought that way, if you think about it. The natives here were essentially still living in the Stone Age. They hadn't even developed bronze. They hadn't invented the wheel. They didn't know about

Jesus. Therefore, they were considered sub-humans. That mentality persisted for a long time, just as it did for some other minorities.

"The European invasion was also a clash between two seemingly incompatible cultures. The Europeans had established a system of land ownership. For the natives, it varied. If they occupied a place where they could sustain an existence, they stayed. But if conditions changed—a drought, a shift in game movement, encroachment from another tribe—they moved. There were always other options because the land was so vast.

"They must have spent a lot of time and effort just finding enough food to keep them alive. Some of them grew crops, usually corn, squash, and beans of some kind. Some ate more fish than anything else, especially on the Pacific coast. Some hunted buffalo, although it's hard to imagine how they did that with no horses until the Spaniards arrived in the 16th century. Some were essentially hunter-gatherers. They must have maintained a running battle with starvation, especially in the winter months. Mother Nature doesn't provide a whole lot that humans can digest in the colder climates.

"Estimates of the pre-Columbian population of North America vary widely. There is no way to know how many natives lived here. But one factor which reduced their numbers more than any other was their lack of immunity to previously unknown diseases. Much of this goes back to the domestication of animals. Only a limited number of animals in the world can be domesticated, and those had already been identified thousands of years ago. Ironically, the horse and the camel originated in North America and emigrated long ago across what is now the Bering Strait to Asia. While the Asians and the Europeans domesticated horses, cattle, sheep, poultry, and many others, the only animal which the natives here could domesticate was the dog from the wolf, except for South American llamas and alpacas. They couldn't domesticate a deer or a buffalo. So while the Europeans were living in close contact with their animals, the natives lacked nearly all of them. They had no mounts or beast of burden. Eventually, diseases from the animals were absorbed by the Europeans, but over time they developed some immunity. However, when they invaded other lands, there was no immunity, and their diseases decimated indigenous populations. A European might survive small pox; a native would almost inevitably die from it. Europeans had also developed some resistance to the effects of alcohol, but natives elsewhere had much less tolerance for it. This has created another serious problem, as you probably know.

"And so we find a somewhat more sophisticated group of people invading what they considered an inferior order, not accepting the latter as equivalent human beings, and bringing with them deadly diseases. The result was predictably catastrophic for the natives. The U.S. government dealt with the Indian problem by trying either to eradicate them or to move them out of the way of progress. In so doing, the negotiators made a series of agreements with people who could not read or comprehend all the terms of the documents. Beyond that, there was a repeated failure of government representatives to honor the treaties. This led to further friction which persists up to the present.

"Today we find the U.S. and Canadian governments trying to deal with over five hundred separate tribal units speaking many different languages while trying to redress a litany of past grievances and broken promises. The bureaucrats have often failed to take the trouble to recognize distinctions among the various tribes. It's almost always a mistake to generalize about a large number of people. The situation has been so badly mishandled in the past that it seems unlikely that anyone will find a mutually acceptable solution. The band-aid solution has been to grant some tribes casino rights, so they can find a quick fix to their grinding poverty. Many natives are struggling to preserve their ancient heritages and languages just as they are trying to find their place in a society which has marginalized them for five centuries. They seem to be caught between two worlds. They have one foot in the past and one in the present, or so it seems."

The four men were quiet for a while, then asked me questions which I did my best to answer from my limited knowledge of the subject. However, I had to confess that I didn't know much about the system of Indian reservations or how they came to be established in the first place.

14

Nobody was looking forward to the prospect of spending another week on the road. The Alaska Highway was at least scenic, but we had already seen it once from the reverse angle. We debated whether to stop in Whitehorse and see the revue again. With no consensus, we decided to wait until we got there and see how we felt by then. We weren't even sure we could get tickets.

We had to stop at the Alaska-Yukon border before returning to Canada. It was a fairly perfunctory procedure, but one aspect of it caught our attention. The Canadian border guards wanted to make sure that we had enough money to make it all the way across their country. That raised an interesting question. If we had come up short, what would our options have been? If we had lacked the financial resources to drive across Canada, we would hardly have had enough to return to a port or airport and book passage. I could understand the Canadians' reluctance to want to add us to their welfare roll, but it was perplexing to imagine how they could just leave someone in limbo, so to speak. Maybe that was what had happened to the campground thieves. We could only speculate. The later proliferation of credit cards must have eliminated that possible dilemma.

We stopped for the night north of Mount Logan and admired it again. It towered more than a mile higher than the highest peak in Wyoming. I realize that there are higher mountains in the world, but none could be more impressive than this one. Looking at it, one could just imagine how the native people must have revered it.

After supper, Uncle Mac pressed me for the next Decameron topic for our game. I replied that since the last two had been rather somber, we needed a little comedy relief. I therefore proposed that each tell about something funny that had happened to him while in the line of duty.

When we reached Whitehorse, we decided to attend the revue again, and we were able to get tickets. We still enjoyed it, but it seemed less entertaining the second time. We already knew what was coming. The next morning we took on water, drained the waste tank, and bought sufficient supplies for the long trek to Dawson Creek. Someone suggested that the Molson brewery owed us special recognition.

❖

Before long someone mentioned that it was time for some diversion, and we should follow through and relate something humorous that had occurred in an otherwise humorless career. Two of them were ready.

> Karl Schultz: Remember I told you about the shift supervisor who thought it was funny to pair Martin with Lewis and Black with White. Well, Black and White, who actually got along remarkably well, decided to put one over on their boss. They waited until April first—April Fools' Day—to pull it. They went into the rest room to prepare. Then White, who was black, smeared flour all over his face, and Black, who was white, darkened his face with burnt

> cork, like they used to do in minstrel shows. Then they came out as if nothing were unusual. Everyone caught the gag right away, and we all cracked up. The sarge just about wet his pants when he first saw them. Our captain came out to see what all the ruckus was about. It took him a minute to get it, but then he started laughing, too. I don't think anyone got much work done the rest of the day.

We all got a good laugh out of the story as well. Then it was Ben Randall's turn:

> We had to respond to 911 calls, but some of them turned out to be frivolous or misguided. The dispatcher tried to sort those out, but sometimes one would slip through. One of those came from an elderly woman who insisted that she had an emergency and needed help. My partner and I rushed to her assistance and found that her "emergency" was that she couldn't get the lid off a new jar of mayonnaise. I looked at my partner, and he looked back at me. I grasped the jar with both hands while he made a big show of straining to turn the lid. After a while, we had accomplished our mission. The troublesome jar was open. The lady informed us that she had arthritis in her hands and had difficulty with tight lids. We suddenly found the situation less than humorous. The poor woman did have what to her was an emergency. She thanked us for our assistance as we left. Neither of us laughed.

Nor did we.

Since the weather report on the radio was calling for more rain, someone suggested that we take a stretch break and eat lunch before continuing on our journey. We stopped by a small lake and went for a short walk. Before long, a swarm of mosquitoes had found our range, and we quickly decided to move the party back inside the RV. We had bought some really good rye bread in Whitehorse to use to make sandwiches with our smoked salmon. We were just starting to get a little tired of our fish diet, but I reminded the others that many of the natives up here had eaten little else all their lives. Karl Schultz made a face and quipped, "Didn't they ever order a pizza?"

It started to rain shortly after we left the lake, and it was Bill Roberts' turn to tell a story:

> I have another 911 tale. Back before I became a detective, my partner and I were patrolling one Saturday afternoon when a call came in. The dispatcher said that a child had called to report that his daddy was hurting his mommy. There was no way to confirm it, so we turned on the siren and hurried to the address. It was a small one-family house with a car parked in the driveway. I rang the doorbell while my partner stayed back a few steps in case there was a violent reaction. I was surprised when a woman in a bathrobe answered the door. When I told her that we were investigating a report of domestic violence, her face turned red with embarrassment. She told us that she and her husband had left their five-year-old son to watch TV while they went into the bedroom. Apparently they had gotten a little carried away and

made some noise, but it wasn't of an abusive nature. I tried not to grin and assured her that we would not be filing a report.

Karl Schultz grinned and commented, "Don't you just love happy endings?"

Uncle Mac had the last laugh: You remember that during the Fifties there was a lot of emphasis on the space program. The U.S. and the USSR were in a dog fight to see who could get to the moon first. The incident at Roswell, New Mexico, had people worried that we were being invaded from Mars. UFO sightings were being reported all over. The motion picture industry cashed in on it by making movies like "The Day the Earth Stood Still." Well, one day our precinct in Chicago received an anonymous phone call from someone who claimed to have found a dead Martian. After he had given the location, he hung up without giving his name. The one who took the call assumed that it was just a hoax, but she reported it, and her supervisor told the dispatcher to have the nearest car go to the reported site just to make sure. Two of our guys went there and found a small cluster of people standing around something. The pair made their way through them and found a very small creature in a shiny yellow space suit with assorted items that looked like something that astronauts might need in an unfamiliar environment. The creature appeared to be dead, but nobody wanted to touch it. One of the cops called their supervisor from the car radio while

> the other one kept the onlookers from getting too close. By the end of the day, we had the entire area cordoned off while we waited for someone from Washington to arrive. Our chief persuaded the news agencies to suppress the news until the facts could be confirmed. He didn't want to start a panic. In remarkably short time, the team from Washington arrived. I don't know what agency they represented. It didn't take them long to solve the mystery. At about the same time, a student from the university called a reporter to tell what he and his friends had done. They had removed a dead monkey from the biology lab and kept it frozen while someone made a little space suit out of yellow satin. One of them bought some convincing-looking space paraphernalia from a toy store. Then they thawed out the monkey, shaved it, cut off its tail, and dressed it in the yellow suit. One of them took it to a little-used part of the park and left it there while another called the police. They hadn't expected the prank to go so far, but they were unrepentant. They hadn't broken any law that carried serious consequences. The local media had some fun with it, and the guys in our precinct made up space monkey stories for quite a while.

Ben Randall responded as he shook his head, "It's amazing what some people will do just to get a laugh."

15

We stopped for gas at Fort Nelson, but didn't see any reason to stay any longer than we had to, especially with it raining. After we had left, Karl Schultz asked for the next Decameron topic so they could be thinking about it. I had an idea which I had been mulling around in my head. I asked them, "With twenty-five years of police service, there must have been some times when you crossed the line—did something that was less than proper police procedure. How would you feel about airing it?"

They were all quiet for some time. Uncle Mac was the first to respond. "You're right, of course. I doubt if any serious cop has played by the book for an entire career. Sometimes the rules of the game leave you disadvantaged. It's like a boxing match where one fighter has to follow Marquis of Queensbury rules, and the other is allowed to bite and kick. The first guy is at a big disadvantage. So once in a while he tries to even the odds a little."

The others nodded in agreement.

Mac continued, "I'd be willing to mention a few incidents, but only if the rest of you promise to keep them confidential. Off hand, I can think of two guys in prison who might have grounds for an appeal if someone found out how we put them where they belong."

Karl Schultz added, "Another thought is that we could

lose our pensions for misconduct if internal affairs ever got after us."

Ben Randall commented, "Now I'm curious to know what you did and if it's any worse than what I did. I'd like to hear this. I'm in."

Bill Roberts concluded, "I'll go along with it, but only under the condition that Mac suggested. None of us mentions this to anyone else as long as we're alive. That goes for you, too, Professor."

I confirmed my part of the deal. And so began a series of stories that I've guarded for over twenty-five years. The four didn't need much time for contemplation.

> Bill Roberts: When the Miranda law came in, I was one of those who strongly opposed it. When I was growing up, my mother told me repeatedly that ignorance of the law is no excuse. That made sense to me, and I never questioned it. The Miranda law changed that. Now a case would be thrown out if we failed to inform a suspect of his rights, which they all knew anyway. Well, shortly after the Miranda law went into effect, my partner and I caught a car thief. Someone reported that his new car had been stolen, and we spotted it cruising down the street. We pulled it over and told the driver to step out. My partner read him the Miranda spiel from a card—we hadn't memorized it yet—and we took him in. During the whole arrest, he looked guilty as sin, but he didn't say anything. He remained silent during the entire booking and fingerprinting procedure. Shortly after we locked him up, a lawyer arrived. He was a pro bono advocate for Hispanics, mostly

Mexicans. After talking to his client, he informed us that our arrest was invalid because the man only knew Spanish and couldn't understand the recitation of his rights. I didn't understand much Spanish, but my partner did, and besides we could tell from his body language that he understood us. Just as the lawyer was about to leave, my partner leaned to me and said in a low voice, "I guess we'll just have to take him out back and shoot him." The man showed instant alarm and shouted, "No!" I grinned at the lawyer and said, "Well, Counselor, there went your case."

Karl Schultz: I remember when two of our guys brought in a kid who had been arrested for shoplifting. He had gone into a discount store and headed for the shoe department. They didn't have any sales clerks there to assist just then, so he tried on some expensive sports shoes by himself. Then he left his old sneakers there and walked away wearing the new ones. Someone saw him and reported it. The store detective followed him out the door and grabbed him. The store manager called the police, and two of us picked him up. You'd expect a youngster like him to be scared or at least apologetic, but this kid was neither. He had been arrested at least three previous times for shoplifting, and he knew that we could do nothing with an under-age offender except refer him to juvenile court, and he had been there before. His mother had given up on him, and his father wasn't in the picture. When we tried to question him, he let us know that we couldn't put him in jail, and his record would be erased after a while. But we were all tired and overworked and not in the mood to take a lot of smart talk from a punk kid. We closed the door to the interrogation room and pulled the blinds. Then two of us held him while another cop pulled the kid's pants down, took off his uniform belt, and gave the punk about ten good swats across his bare butt. He was careful not to leave a mark, but it was hard enough to be effective. The kid bawled and spouted some obscenities, but his bravado was gone. I made sure that he knew he'd better not make a return appearance by telling him that if he came back to us, we'd see to it that he stayed in reform school until he was twenty-one. I was a little concerned that he might report us, but one of the older cops theorized that the kid would be too ashamed to tell anyone that he'd received a spanking. I don't know what became of him because we never saw him again. I'd like to think that he learned something that day.

Uncle Mac: This was an odd one. I had to go to Geneva, out on the west end of the Chicago area, to represent my department at a conference on mutual cooperation. After the meeting was over, one of the cops there, his name was Martin, offered me a ride to the restaurant where we were to have supper. Just after we'd started out, he received a radio call about a hit-and-run. A witness had seen a car run a red light and hit a bicyclist, then take off without stopping. The observer was able to get a license number, and it appeared that the car was headed our way. Sure enough, the car came right by us. Martin turned on his siren and gave chase. The guy just sped up and headed west out of town. He probably thought that we wouldn't follow him, but we did. A few miles down the road, he turned into the driveway of an old farm, which appeared to be abandoned. We followed him in and were surprised to see the driver get out of the car. We were even more surprised to see that "he" was a middle-aged woman. As we approached her, she tried to appear calm. Her game plan was to tell us that we had no jurisdiction there, which was true. But Martin had already thought of that. He told her that we would call the county sheriff and have him arrest her. The woman continued to be defiant and seemed to be oblivious to the seriousness of her situation. We could see the marks on her car and knew that she had no defense other than the question of jurisdiction. We knew that if we left her alone, she could get rid of the car. So Martin proposed something unorthodox. He had me help him handcuff her to a fence and told her that he would call the sheriff and tell him where the key was. We left her sputtering and returned to Geneva for supper. What he didn't tell her was that it might take a while for him to call the sheriff. It was late spring and not dangerously cold, but chilly enough to be uncomfortable. Martin knew the sheriff and felt that he could count on his support. He called me later and told me that the sheriff had reached the woman around midnight, by which time she had wet her pants and lost most of her bluster. Fortunately for her, the bicyclist had survived, thus sparing her a charge of vehicular homicide.

Ben Randall: While I was with the Nebraska state police, we used to patrol rural areas a lot. Out in some of the small towns there isn't a lot of serious crime, but sometimes bored teen-agers get their kicks by committing petty vandalism, like smashing mail boxes with baseball bats. To me, vandalism is one of the most mindless of all crimes. It gains the perpetrator nothing and irritates the victim a lot. If I live to be a hundred, I'll never understand it. But it happens. Well, one summer there was a rash of such incidents in Custer County. Someone was hitting mail boxes, letting cattle out of their pasture, spray-painting barns, and generally creating mischief. We asked the people in the area to be on the look-out, since we couldn't cover the whole county. Sure enough, someone spotted four kids in an old Chevy playing their game late at night. When we found out who they were, it wasn't hard to catch them. We pulled them over one night. My senior partner had some entertainment arranged for them. He took two of them in the patrol car, and I drove the Chevy with the other two to a remote dirt road. There he made them take their clothes off, leaving only their shoes. He told them where they could find their clothes and the Chevy, and we left them there. I'd guess they had about a ten-mile walk ahead of them. Afterward I wondered what we would have done if there had been any girls with them. It would have been a different plan, but I don't know what it would have been.

The rest of us chuckled at the story, but then Uncle Mac spoke. "It has been entertaining to hear about stories like this, and maybe it did us some good to tell them. But it has been obvious that we each started with a fairly innocuous story. I'm sure that each of us has been involved in a more flagrant incident than those which we just told. Think about it, and we'll see what the next round brings."

16

We made slow progress over the next stretch of road because of frost heaves—waves in the highway caused by the freezing and thawing of the ground. We eventually came to a long stretch between ranges where we could actually drive faster than fifty miles an hour without worrying about running off the road. We met several gravel trucks heading toward some rough spots in the road. Even though it was paved, their short-term solution for maintenance was to throw some coarse gravel on it. Wild life still was not as abundant as we had expected. We only saw a moose or two about every hundred miles or so, usually a cow with a calf, and we never did see a wolf.

We stopped at a rest stop which housed an information center regarding the highway. We had skipped it on the way up. It provided a rather detailed explanation of the construction of the Al-Can Highway, complete with numerous photos and maps. It was impressive. Having just traveled the entire length of the highway, we were in a good position to appreciate the enormity of the undertaking.

Before we set out again, I proposed another topic. I said, "While you're trying to decide which breach of etiquette you want to disclose next, how about telling us a little about your various partners? You've referred to them often enough. I'd like to hear a little more about them. That shouldn't take any preparation."

The four consented rather half heartedly, and Ben Randall began:

I had two different partners in Kansas City before I was promoted to lieutenant. The first was an older guy named Peterson. He didn't talk much, and I'm not much better, so I never got to know him very well. He liked to remind me that he had a son who was nearly my age. After he retired, I was paired with his exact opposite. His name was Curtis, and he talked non-stop. Some of the other cops liked to kid him, because he was slow to figure out when they were serious and when they weren't. One of the guys faked a Brooklyn accent and started calling him "Coitus." He didn't know what it meant until somebody clued him in. I thought he might get mad, but he thought it was funny. Since he had a family and I didn't, we didn't socialize much. He was all right as a partner. We got through a few scrapes together. When I was promoted to lieutenant and wouldn't be working with a partner anymore, he took me out for a beer after work one evening. I seldom saw him after that.

Karl Schultz: I've already mentioned getting into a bar fight with my partner and me against five guys. His name was Pat O'Donnell, and he was my partner for twenty years. The two of us represented the main source of American cops for at least a century. He was Irish, and I'm German. During the nineteenth century a lot of Irish and Germans immigrants came to America because conditions were really bad back in the old countries. But over here, they faced discrimination as the latest poor folks off the boat. A lot of the men took jobs on the police force or joined the Army because they couldn't find work anywhere else. So in a way, we were the personifications of a stereotype. But aside from that, we were not only partners, we were also best friends. His wife and mine got along well, and so we took turns hosting Sunday dinners. It probably wasn't fair because they had three kids and we didn't have any, but we didn't care. Their kids called us Aunt Helga and Uncle Karl, and we remembered all their birthdays until they grew up. Sadly, O'Donnell had a heart attack and died just before he was to retire. His wife moved away to be closer to her family, and we didn't hear from her very often after that. I still miss them.

Uncle Mac: I had several partners. The first was an Italian named Giovanni, which is usually a first name, but it was his last name. He was about my age. He was a good cop, and we got along. But he had some notion about joining the Secret Service, and eventually he made it. The next one didn't last long. I can't even remember his name. He had a drinking problem, and it eventually cost him his job. Then there was Gonzales. Most Mexicans weren't big enough to meet the size standard, but he was about six feet tall and well built. He could take care of himself in just about any situation. We got along all right, but we didn't socialize much. He was close to his extended family and spent most of his off-duty time with them. I usually spent most of mine with one girl friend or another, as you already know.

My last partner was a woman. They had just started assigning women to patrol duty, and they broke up Gonzales and me and gave us both female partners. My new partner's name was Gladys Wilson. She was as big as most men, but still fairly attractive. She was only about ten years younger than I. She was competent and dedicated enough, and I was losing my concern about having a female partner. At the same time, I was enough of a red-blooded American male to be interested in her after duty. She took me up on offers to go out for a beer after work twice, but usually she declined. I think I must have been the last one in the precinct to realize that she liked girls better than boys. After that, I just treated her like any other partner. She held up her end of the bargain, and I did the same, and we got along just fine. I probably should have left it at that in the first place. Romantic involvement can get in the way of a professional relationship.

Bill Roberts: Since I was a detective and not a beat cop, I never had an assigned partner for long. It wasn't like the TV shows. My alter ego, Joe Friday, always had a partner, but I didn't. We were assigned to various task forces according to the mission. I might have worked with a forensics specialist on one assignment and a dog handler on the next. But once I worked with a computer whiz for quite a while. He was a young guy named Wright. He was fresh out of the University of Colorado. He had been hired

> to track down computer hackers. Computers were brand new then, and most of us didn't have a clue about them. But this guy knew all about them and was particularly useful because he had been a hacker. He hadn't done anything illegal, though. He and a few of his classmates had just found it amusing to see if they could break into a secure system and leave a silly message, like "Kilroy was here." He helped us catch several hackers whose main purpose was to steal personal information and sell it to anyone who had an unauthorized use for that kind of data. He was chagrinned, though, when we used his input to arrest one of his former classmates, but he got over it.

That was an interesting interlude, but I reminded the four that after they had talked about their latest revelations, I made an observation. I said, "After thinking about your latest round of 'true confessions,' I've noticed that some of you were more willing to talk about breaches of protocol that you've witnessed than any which you may have committed. I suggest that we focus on more of those before we get down to the ones in which you played a more active role."

No one objected to my proposal. They were still clearly reluctant to go too far with their admissions.

17

We had mixed feelings when we arrived back in Dawson Creek. We were relieved to have survived three thousand miles of Alaska Highway with no mishap, but we would miss the wild beauty of the landscape. The adventure was over. All that was left was a rather boring long ride back out of Canada. Just to be different, we went to a pizza parlor for supper.

The boredom of the next stretch was relieved by a flat front tire. It took us over an hour to figure out how to change a tire on a Winnebago, but we managed to get it done. We were just glad that it wasn't raining for a change.

As we were approaching the prairie, it started to rain again. It was no wonder that everything was so green. But the inclement weather helped us to focus on the discussions inside the RV. The topic was roughly observations of someone else crossing the line.

> Ben Randall started the next round: This happened while I was still working in rural Nebraska. A drifter hooked up with a young single woman who had an eight-year-old daughter. This kind of story seems to play out too often. Boyfriend lusts after girlfriend's young daughter. One day the mother came home from work to find out that the creep had raped and beaten the little girl, then taken off. The woman

called the police, and they put out an APB on him. Some of the locals heard about it and they joined in the chase. As luck would have it, the guy's old car died a few miles down the road. He tried to take off on foot, but some of the posse caught up with him. As I understand it, he "resisted arrest" for quite a while, but eventually they brought him back into town. There he "resisted arrest" some more while they were waiting for one of our guys to show up. By the time he stopped resisting arrest, he was a better candidate for the hospital than the jail. The court appointed a lawyer to defend him. There was no question about his guilt, but the lawyer tried to appeal for clemency on the grounds that the other prisoners would abuse him. It's well known that "baby rapers" rank at the bottom of the food chain in prison. But no one was sympathetic. If someone had organized a lynch mob, probably half the town would have brought ropes. I don't know what became of him, and frankly I don't care. I doubt if that girl ever recovered completely from that. She'd be over thirty by now. I think of her every so often.

Uncle Mac: I have a story that's similar to the one Ben told about the Nebraska vandals. A couple of cops from southern Illinois told me this one. There was a used car salesman down there who had a serious drinking problem. He had been arrested for DWI several times, I forget how many. His driver's license had been revoked, but he kept driving anyway. His boss was also his brother-in-law, so he managed to keep his job and find a car to drive. The legal system didn't seem to have the means to stop him until he hurt someone, and that just appeared to be a matter of time. Well, our colleagues decided not to wait for that to happen. A few short stays in jail hadn't made much difference to him, so our guys planned something extra. The next time they caught him weaving down the road, they took him for a ride down a dead-end gravel road. But unlike the treatment that Ben described, they left him his clothes, but took his shoes. Then they left him there with a note pinned to his shirt. It told him in rather graphic terms what would happen to him if he ever tried to drive without a license again, with a bonus effect if he were caught drunk behind the wheel. Apparently that got his attention. They never had to arrest him again.

Karl Schultz: We had a big problem with a drug ring. That was maybe five or six years ago. We could catch some of the small fish, but we wanted the big operators. Finally we caught one who was high enough up the ladder to give us some vital information, but he was smart enough to know how far we could go to make him talk. He hinted that he wanted to make a deal with us on his own terms, but the higher-ups of the ring had called in an expensive lawyer whose main function was to make sure that he didn't say anything that might involve them. Our DA didn't want to make a deal and gave us tacit approval to try a little harder to get the information. One of our guys came up with an unorthodox idea. He knew that the lawyer wouldn't want to work on the weekend, and most of our people would be off. We were also prohibited from questioning a suspect without the presence of his lawyer. So they just left the guy locked in the interrogation room for the weekend. He had no food or water and just a waste basket for a toilet. They didn't have to lay a hand on him. By Monday morning he was more than ready to talk. He told us all we wanted to know and then some.

Bill Roberts: About three years ago we caught an investment broker who had set up a Ponzi scheme and bilked a lot of people out of their savings. He had focused on older people because they usually had more assets. I was there when they brought him in. I was amazed at how unrepentant he was. To him it was all just a game. As long as he could promise eventual restitution, there was no problem, at least in his warped mind. He just seemed to regard his arrest as a minor set-back. He hadn't lost his family because his wife and grown son obviously knew what he was doing, and they had been enjoying the fruits of his labor, so to speak. He already had a law firm on retainer, and two of the lawyers appeared at his arraignment. They persuaded the judge to release him on bail pending trial. They appeared confident. Some of the elderly victims of the scheme were there in the courtroom, and they were outraged. The accused looked right past them as he left the courtroom. But he had underestimated the magnitude of their anger. Two days later someone set his house on fire while nobody was there. It was a total loss, and

> his home owner's insurance didn't cover arson. The fire department conducted an investigation, and our department checked for other evidence, but no one came up with any conclusive leads. I really doubt if anyone was very serious about finding out who was responsible.

The four had more stories to tell because each one reminded them of a similar episode. That kept them occupied for several hours while we continued toward Edmonton.

18

By the time we reached Edmonton, we had run out of fish to eat. Uncle Mac suggested that we treat ourselves to a steak dinner, which met with unanimous approval. We also needed to tend to the maintenance of the Winnebago as well as our personal hygiene. We found a campground where we could drain our waste water, fill our water tank, refill the propane tank, and take showers. In accordance with our agreement, none of us had shaved on the trip. Ben Randall had the thickest beard; I had the sparsest. We all looked like refugees from a western movie—or a chain gang. By then we had traveled far enough south for the nights to be dark for a few hours, which improved our ability to sleep. Soon our adventure would be over. But we still had two long days on the road ahead of us.

As we departed from Edmonton the next morning, I mentioned that it was time for the four to tell the most personal of the stories: When did you cross the line of acceptable police procedure? Nobody wanted to start, and I could still sense a certain reluctance from them to reveal a rather dark secret. Therefore, I made an alternative suggestion. I said, "Why don't you take another day to think about it. Meanwhile, here's an easier topic. I'm sure you all have opinions about this one. One of you already mentioned it: What do you think of the American Civil Liberties Union—the ACLU?"

At that, all of them wanted to talk, but my uncle won the contest to begin.

Uncle Mac: I never thought much about them one way or the other until that episode a few years ago, when the American Nazi Party filed for permission to stage a parade down the streets of Skokie, which has a large Jewish population. The media had a field day with it, because a lot of people were outraged. The ACLU came out with the position that the Nazis had a First Amendment right to assemble, as long as it was done peacefully. The police were considerably less than thrilled with the idea of keeping such an event peaceful. The whole mess went to court, and a judge ruled that there was no legal reason to deny the Nazi request. No matter how distasteful the proposition was to the vast majority of people, the ACLU position had the backing of the Constitution. We all braced for the worst, but the Nazis withdrew their request voluntarily. They probably knew that, law or no law, they would be in for a lot of grief if they tried such an outrageous stunt. Since then, I've had little sympathy for the ACLU. I think they have good intentions, but they tend to go off the deep end.

Ben Randall: I'm inclined to agree. I think they have something in common with the NRA, which likes to invoke the Second Amendment right to bear arms. I've carried a weapon for most of my life, but I don't have an unlimited right to be armed. If I commit a felony, I lose that right. If I try to board a plane carrying a loaded shotgun, someone will probably object. There are practical limits to all of our rights. We just don't all agree on what they should be, and the ACLU tends to stress the literal interpretation of the documents.

Bill Roberts: I mentioned the police captain who was criticized by the ACLU for being too quick on the trigger, in their view. I could see their point, up to a degree. We're only supposed to use force as a last resort. But when you're in a life-threatening situation, you don't have a lot of time to weigh the options. I was fortunate enough to have avoided most of those, but I have a lot of admiration for the people who have looked death in the face and reacted bravely. I have great respect for that captain. I have nothing but contempt for his critics.

I'm also reminded of my time in the Army. All of us relinquished some of our rights when we joined the military. We quickly learned to do as we were told and not worry too much about the justice of it. In times of emergency, curfews can be imposed in the interest of public safety. In extreme cases, martial law can be mandated. That cancels out just about any notion of individual rights. I'll bet the ACLU would have a field day with that.

Karl Schultz: Twice in my life I've taken oaths to defend the Constitution of the United States of America. I realize that it's a wonderful document and has been the model for several others, but I get disturbed when I hear someone ask what the

> Founding Fathers intended when they wrote it. I have great respect and admiration for the men who put it together, but they lived two hundred years ago in a very different world. I don't think that what they intended is necessarily very relevant to us. We should be interpreting it according to the conditions of today. Just consider Ben's example about the right to bear arms. They had single-shot firearms back then and faced some dangers that are no longer present. We have automatic and semi-automatic weapons that have no practical use except in warfare. How do we compare those situations?
>
> But getting back to the ACLU, they're mainly focused on the First Amendment to the Constitution. I know that it's primarily concerned with our right to the freedoms of speech, the press, religion, assembly, but does anyone remember the exact wording?

I replied, "I had to memorize it for civics class in high school: 'Congress shall make no law respecting an establishment of religion, or prohibiting the free exercise thereof; or abridging the freedom of speech or the press; or the right of the people peaceably to assemble, and to petition the Government for a redress of grievances.'"

Uncle Mac responded, "OK, Professor, let's hear your opinion on the subject. What do you think of the ACLU?"

I was surprised and a little flattered to be included in the discussion for the first time. Up to then, I had only provided academic information. I drew a deep breath as I started.

"The ACLU seems to take the most literal interpretation of the First Amendment. I would maintain that there are, and always have been, limits to all of our freedoms. Take freedom of speech. When we started school, we quickly learned that our freedom of speech was limited by the teacher's tolerance level. I still remember as a seven-year-old having to stay after school and write repeatedly on the blackboard, 'I will raise my hand before I speak.' So much for my freedom of speech. If we engage in a discussion during a movie or performance, we will probably be invited to practice our freedom of speech elsewhere. If we exercise complete freedom of expression at work, we may find that our supervisor has limited patience for our observations. Total candor might not be the wisest career move.

"We have a degree of freedom of the press that is unparalleled in much of the world. We might extend that to the other media, since the electronic forms hadn't been invented yet two hundred years ago. In countries ruled by dictators, anything critical of the government can result in severe consequences. In some countries, the government controls all the media. We can express our opinions on just about any subject without fear of punishment. But there are limits. There are laws relating to libel and slander. We may only go so far.

"Few countries enjoy the religious freedom that we do. We may believe just about anything--or nothing--without fear of being arrested or burnt at the stake for heresy. We take that for granted, but it was not always so. There are some rather nasty chapters in the history of Christianity, such as the Inquisition, which even the most devout of us would rather forget. In some parts of the world, the religious institutions are not far removed from the Inquisition. However, I'm not aware that the ACLU has had occasion to deal much with religion.

"Freedom of assembly is usually guaranteed, but not always. The key word is 'peaceably,' and that is subject to interpretation. The Nazi parade in Skokie was approved as long as it was conducted peaceably. The marches in Alabama during the Sixties were curtailed because someone judged them as disruptive. It's a matter of opinion as to where a demonstration becomes a riot.

"It seems that our First Amendment freedoms are subject to some interpretation. It's clear to me that we are not free to say or print just anything, nor may we push the limits of peaceful assemble. The ACLU tends to support the literal interpretation of the First Amendment. I would prefer to see it tempered with some degree of common sense. There have always been limits to our freedom. Realistically, there should be."

A lively discussion ensued all the way to Saskatoon.

19

We had waited until the last day of the trip to address the final question: When did you cross the line? We were almost back to Manitoba before everyone settled down to deal with the toughest item on the agenda.

> Karl Schultz started with a preamble: It has been my experience that the vast majority of police work consists of dealing with minor offenses. A lot of those just reflect poor judgment. Someone had a heavy foot on the gas pedal or tried to beat a red light. We give a lot of warnings and traffic tickets to those people, but their offenses are usually fairly harmless. At the next level are the petty law-breakers: the shoplifters, the window peepers, the small-time thieves, the flashers, the recreational drug users. From there it escalates through robbery, drug dealing, battery, rape, and manslaughter. Here we're starting to talk serious prison time. But at the top of the list are some people out there who are just plain evil. They would do anything for the right price, and they seem to lack any kind of conscience. They would kill a rival or anyone else who threatens them. Some just kill for no apparent reason. When we deal with people like that, we are sometimes thwarted by a system that seems to show more

concern for legal technicalities than for the right of all the rest of us to keep people like that off the streets. Right now the taxpayers are shelling out a lot of money to keep some of those folks locked up. But there are plenty more of them out there, and as cops we had to deal with them. Some of our stories will show our frustration at having guidelines which were designed for more ordinary people, not the sociopaths.

Karl continued: Some of the gangsters are the worst. If the thugs aren't already total reprobates, they usually develop that way. I'm not talking about motorcycle gangs or ethnic gangs. Most of those are just young guys showing off, and they outgrow it. I mean the ones connected with organized crime. Once they're in, it's almost impossible for them to get out alive, even if they want to. Most of those that I clashed with were into the drug business. It's fairly easy money without the risk that goes with robbing banks or armored cars. Their biggest threat usually comes from rival gangs. They do a lot of our work for us by eliminating each other.

A few years ago, we tried to use the bad blood between two gangs against each other. One had ties to Las Vegas, and the other with Miami. They weren't considered important enough to attract the FBI, so we were on our own. We arrested one of them, questioned him, and let it slip that the other gang was feeding us information about his gang. Then we released him, supposedly for insufficient evidence. After that, we had a long discussion about just how far off the track we were prepared to go, and we made a grim agreement. We decided to stir up the pot by shooting a member of his gang. I did it. I had a 30.06 hunting rifle with a scope and plugged one of them from about 300 yards. His cohorts assumed that the other gang had done it. Before long, we had a regular gang war going on. They did quite a number on each other. That gave us a reason to move in officially. By the time we raided them, there were only about half as many to deal with. What we did was well beyond the scope of our authority, but it was effective, and it saved the taxpayers a lot of money for trials. I wouldn't recommend doing it again, though. If the DA's office ever finds out about it, there could still be some nasty repercussions.

Ben Randall: We had a fairly large prostitution operation going in Kansas City about ten years ago. Nobody got too excited about it as long as there was no major outbreak of venereal disease and it appeared to be consentual all around. But then we learned that someone was recruiting under-aged girls from Mexico. Since most of them were here illegally, they were afraid to complain if they were mistreated. One of our female cops volunteered to go in undercover—if that's an acceptable term for it—to try to find out what was going on and who was responsible. She was able to confirm our worst suspicions. Girls as young as thirteen were being brought in, sometimes after having been sold by their destitute parents. But while she was trying to gain more information, they found out who she was, and she paid the full price. We found her battered body in a dumpster. That set off the nastiest round of reprisals I've ever seen. We used the information she had provided to make two big raids. If there was ever a "take no prisoners!" scenario, that was it. We just waded in and opened fire on them. I did my share. The only reason I didn't kill anyone was because somebody else beat me to it. After it was over, we all expected to be suspended or worse, but we didn't care. But guess what! Nobody filed any kind of a complaint against us. People who kill cops don't get the least bit of sympathy from any quarter.

Bill Roberts: My story isn't all that exciting. I was a detective for most of my career and didn't tangle with any gangs. When I crossed the line, it was usually when I lost my temper. One night I was called to investigate a robbery. Someone had reported a break-in at a jewelry store, and I just happened to be the closest to the scene. As I approached the store, someone dressed all in black came running out. I yelled at him, but he wasn't about to stop. I was a pretty good runner, but he had on sneakers, and I was wearing dress shoes. I had to chase him for several blocks before he got tired and I caught up with him. But then he tried to fight me. I was already mad at him for making me chase him, and I beat the crap out of him. I made him walk back to my car, where the radio was. I didn't anticipate any problem, since he hadn't even bothered to get rid of the jewelry in his pocket. But I hadn't counted on an over-eager young defense lawyer. She tried to raise the possibility that I had planted the jewelry on him after we'd had a fight, in which I had used excessive force. There weren't any witnesses, so it was just his word against mine. Fortunately for me, my chief backed me up and got me off the hook. After that, I thought twice about roughing somebody up, and I never got into trouble for using excessive force again.

Uncle Mac: If you recall, I told you about an incident when I was a boy and resisted the temptation to take more money from an elderly woman than I was supposed to. Well, this story has a certain similarity to that one. I was involved in a drug bust. I was on a task force which had been tracking the movements of some major operators. They had been dealing all over the area and had a network of minor dealers, mostly kids who wouldn't do any jail time if they were caught. The feds were in control of the exercise. Indications were that the people we were watching were not of the violent persuasion, but we could never be sure of that. Our sources informed us that the subjects moved around a lot as a safety precaution. Their latest base of operations was an abandoned warehouse on the west side of Chicago. The feds coordinated all movements with us, and we planned to hit it one Sunday morning, when they would least expect it. Sorta like Pearl Harbor.

At the designated time, we came racing in from four directions and tried to cut off any possible escape. When we broke in, there were maybe a dozen people in there, some honchos, some distributors, and they all started running every which way. Soon our carefully laid plan devolved into a Keystone Kops episode. I was among the first ones in, feeling relieved that nobody was shooting at me. As I moved to the center of the building to see what was there, I found a large amount of marijuana. I could smell that as soon as I came in. There was also some kind of substance packaged in plastic which I did not immediately recognize. There was a Volkswagen bus in there, too, presumably preparing to deliver some of the drugs to a dealer. I opened the side door and looked in. Much to my surprise, there were several boxes of cash, all neatly bundled and sorted according to denomination: hundreds, fifties, and twenties. Nothing smaller. Without giving it much thought, I grabbed a bundle of fifties and two of twenties and stuffed them into my jacket. I knew instinctively that hundreds would be harder to spend without creating suspicion. Then I stepped out of the vehicle to see what else was going on. My companions had caught all of the would-be escapees, and the feds were examining the drugs. It took a while for one of them to check out the VW and find the cash. They took charge of both finds, and we chalked up one more victory for the good guys.

I have to admit that I have a certain moral dilemma with my actions that day. On the one hand, I don't see it the same as stealing from someone. It was drug money, after all. On the other hand, I should have left it there to help pay for the national debt or something. I'm ambivalent about it. But on the brighter side, it helped us pay for this trip.

20

Someone mentioned that we had spent the 4th of July in Canada, and that we had seen no fireworks. I'm sure that he was just trying to be funny. It was probably Karl Schultz. That sounds like something that he would have said.

We returned to Minneapolis roughly four weeks after we had left, stopping in Fargo just long enough to confirm our flight reservations by phone. We had driven over nine thousand miles in that time. I would miss the trusty Winnebago RV which had carried us that far with no major mechanical problems. I would not miss the bed I'd been sleeping on. It was not very comfortable.

Karl Schultz, Ben Randall, and Bill Roberts said goodbye when the time came for them to catch their respective flights home. I stayed with Uncle Mac while he drove the RV back to the rental agency and waited while they completed their inspection. Then the agency provided transportation to the airport for us, and we flew back to Chicago together. It was a short flight, only about an hour, and we hadn't finished reminiscing about the trip by the time the plane landed. But we had to part company at O'Hare because we both had a lot of catch-up work to do after having been gone so long.

❖

Over the next twenty-five years, I saw Uncle Mac several times, mostly at family functions. He came to my wedding in 1989, as usual with his latest girl friend. Two years later he astonished all of us by marrying her. My wife and I went to their wedding. By then, we were expecting our first child.

I never saw the other three again, but Uncle Mac stayed in touch with them and kept me informed about them. I sent them Christmas cards for a while, but they never responded, so I gave up. I was disappointed, but that wasn't so unusual. "Out of sight, out of mind," as the saying goes.

Uncle Mac told me that Karl Schultz had taken a part-time job as a bank guard. It had been a rather boring job until two men tried to rob the bank. Karl and one of the robbers had exchanged gun fire, and both had died from their wounds. We didn't find out what his wife did after that.

Bill Roberts had gone into real estate to take advantage of the mass migration to Colorado. His daughter re-established contact with him after she was grown, and he was able to play the role of grandpa to his two grandchildren. He had always been active, and so it was perhaps fitting that he had a heart attack and died while playing golf.

Ben Randall found a new career doing volunteer work in underdeveloped countries. I had to admire him. He went into places which had been devastated by earthquakes, floods, volcanic eruptions, you name it. He was mainly involved in distributing emergency rations and clean water. Unfortunately, those situations were festering grounds for a wide variety of diseases, and one of them claimed him.

I already mentioned that Uncle Mac got married for the first time after I did. As it turned out, his bride was the widow of a very wealthy industrialist and liked to travel. For the next several years they sent us post cards from all over the world. But that all ended when he was diagnosed with pancreatic cancer. He only lived about a year after that.

My life in the last quarter-century has been considerably less exciting than theirs, but I wouldn't change places with any of them. I'm still teaching high school English at the school where I started. My wife works part time at an insurance company. We have a son, who is now trying to decide where he wants to go to college, and a daughter who wants to be a rock star. Three years ago I bought a small used RV and took them all to Alaska. Along the way, I told them about some of the things that had happened on the last trip, but I didn't tell them about the final Decameron stories. I kept my word on that.

"The Professor"

Statistical Testing in Practice with StatsDirect

Research without Tears or Algebra

Cole Davis

Llumina Press

ISBN: 978-1-60594-450-0 (PB)
978-1-60594-451-7 (HC)
978-1-60594-452-4 (EB)

Printed in the United States of America by Llumina Press

Library of Congress Control Number: 2009913282

Contents

Section One:
Background Knowledge

CHAPTER ONE

INTRODUCTION

WHY THIS BOOK WAS WRITTEN

As an applied researcher, I was once asked to produce a training course on computerised statistics for that numerous body of individuals, researchers who do not understand or feel comfortable with statistics. I then found similar needs among the ranks of business people, accountants, the medical profession, civil servants, local government officials and students struggling with academic texts.

I looked for books which could ameliorate this situation and found that many were full of equations, satisfying a statistician's concern with mathematical rigour but repelling the ordinary reader. Others told you more than you needed to know as a beginner, so much so that there was no way of knowing what was important and what was peripheral. The few better books either failed to address the data analysis requirements of the real world – primarily dealing with experimental situations - or told the user how to calculate the statistics by hand. Yet other books attempted to teach both statistics and the use of complex industrial software packages at the same time: one researcher suggested that MSc and PhD students are dropped in at the deep end like this "because it's supposed to be hard".

This is intended to be a short, highly practical book, designed to offer the reader a quick and easy introduction to the analysis of data. Fundamental concepts are presented in the first section – which should be read for a proper understanding of statistical testing – but other ideas are introduced where they logically arise. Each statistical test is accompanied by worked examples which are pertinent to applied research and to basic business problems.

In order to deal with the many practical problems of data analysis without learning how to use tricky information technology at the same time, all the exercises in this book refer to StatsDirect. An excellent but easy-to-use software package, StatsDirect is both inexpensive and allows easy transfer of data to Microsoft Excel spreadsheets. StatsDirect is very rich in features, so the book demonstrates some of the most basic statistical procedures to stop you losing your way.

WHO IS THIS BOOK FOR?

The primary audience is obviously those needing to interpret and analyse data.

Members of this audience may include business personnel who want to add that extra value to what they do. As will be seen, this may include ascertaining whether or not a trend can be said to be significant. It may also involve working out which factors have the most influence on business outcomes.

Other readers may be those involved in applied research, such as interviewing, focus groups and survey questionnaires (also of value to marketers). Social or educational researchers, for example, may want to quantify their findings. Other readers may wish to add to their own market value by acquiring additional skills.

Other potential beneficiaries may be those undertaking research for the first time – for example, as part of a postgraduate project – or returning to research after a break. The case of one of the researchers who spoke to me on these issues is illustrative of both. She said that not only was it a nightmare to learn statistics at the same time as learning a difficult software package, but this flurry of activity had an almost inevitable outcome: she couldn't remember a thing!

People wanting to 'break into' data analysis may do well to start here. If they subsequently want to transfer their understanding to the use of more difficult software, SPSS users could do worse than to advance to *SPSS 12 Made Simple* by Paul R. Kinnear and Colin D. Gray, 2004 (Psychology Press: Hove, East Sussex).

THE PRESENTATION OF CONCEPTS IN THIS BOOK

Coherence, rather than comprehensiveness, is the key to this book. As an applied researcher, I do not feel constrained by the requirements of academic boards, so I am avoiding squiggles and citations of formulae. (Ok, I do use numbers and decimals; into all gardens, some rain must fall.)

I do not think it practical, however, to protect the reader from all statistical jargon: this will be met when using any piece of statistical software, let alone when reading the reports of others, and any other books on statistics. Where appropriate, I introduce alternative names for various concepts; this variegation is reflected in different software packages and books.

Each chapter contains a 'controversy' section, or *'Talking Point'*. These tend to raise issues where the received wisdom may be erroneous or impractical.

The Background Knowledge section should be read in its entirety in order to make full sense of the practical work to come. As statistical testing is primarily about inferential statistics, my introduction to descriptive statistics is speedy and highly selective. But it does have a bearing on the preliminary analysis of data, which should be carried out before running tests. The section on the analysis of differences is fairly conventional, apart from a slight leaning towards non-parametrics as a more useful tool for data analysis 'in the field'. Although possibly a little controversial in its title, the section on qualitative (or categorical) analysis is fairly standard, but a broader set of practical usages is introduced than is usually the case in more academic texts. The section on relationships between data - Correlations, Regression and Factor Analysis - goes beyond some introductory texts in introducing both multiple regression and factor analysis. We need to face the fact that more and more use is made of multiple regression these days and, as will become obvious from the business exercise, it has clear practical advantages. It is often the sorry fate of people faced with PhD projects (amongst others) to find themselves face-to-face with a problem requiring some form of factor analysis technique (I use Principal Components Analysis here) and to discover that 'simple introductions' to these techniques tend to be anything but simple. I hope that the minimalist treatment given here will meet the need for immediate action and will make it easier to absorb more in-depth texts because you will already have acquired a grasp of the essentials.

After covering survival analysis, traditionally used in health research, but with other uses, the book culminates with a section which includes a short set of exercises. Unlike academic tests, exercises do not accompany each section: as practical research is not accompanied by a guide saying 'this problem is one which involves a t-test', it makes more sense to use your overall knowledge from the book to tackle these problems once you have read it through.

The chapter on the presentation of statistics for non-academic purposes is designed to satisfy organisations with practical concerns; readers with academic needs can use this book as a speedy way of gaining a fundamental understanding of statistics, but will need to move to more specific works of reference before writing academic reports. A brief discussion of some other types of statistical tests follows.

Some data sets used for exercises will be reused and built up as the book goes on in order to avoid the need for either lengthy data entry or internet downloads. On the whole, small data sets have been chosen. Through most of the book, two sets of worked examples accompany the tests, with themes which should be of interest to various audiences. It should be noted, however, that statistical principles are applicable to a broad range of disciplines and that readers are encouraged to follow all the exercises with StatsDirect in order to absorb the basic principles.

WHO SHOULDN'T READ THIS BOOK?

Those already comfortable with statistics and in need of extending their knowledge to, for example, multivariate or biological statistics should be looking elsewhere. Those wishing to study for an academic qualification in statistics should really be going to a text specifically targeting that qualification. And, no offence intended, statisticians and mathematicians will probably hate this book – most squiggles are probably typographic errors.

Neither is research design a primary focus of this book. Although some references to this will be made in the theoretical section and a little more at the start of practical sections, they are primarily there to facilitate sensible use of the tests.

Using the Book

This is a short book, and I strongly recommend that you read all of it, preferably completing the exercises as well. If this can't be achieved, I still consider it absolutely necessary to read the theoretical section first, before selecting a chapter and launching straight into a project. Understanding is all.

Readers who later wish to learn more about statistics, including more advanced methods, will be able to do so, confident that they have a grasp of the basic issues involved. Similarly, those who wish to progress to expensive and complicated statistics packages such as SPSS or SAS should be able to do so after having gained useful core experience of data analysis.

A Brief Note About the Author

I was never 'good at mathematics', attaining the school O level (approximate equivalent to the English GCSE) after some retakes. Learning univariate (single variable) statistical tests when studying psychology as an undergraduate at the Open University, I had to do these by hand in those days, spending hours working out formulae without generally seeing the point of the mathematics. As soon as I bought my first computer – a Hitachi which ran with two clunking disk drives and no hard drive – I put the formulae on a spreadsheet and found that the real point was to know which tests to use on what data and what they were useful for, without worrying overmuch about the intermediary equations.

Working on the MSc Occupational Psychology at Birkbeck College, University of London, I deepened my knowledge of applied research and became one of those stressed people attempting to learn about factor analysis for a project at the same time as trying to master SPSS for DOS (the 'black screen' version, using typed commands). Since then, I have become involved in a wide range of research projects, within diverse organisations, extending my understanding *en route*. At the time of writing, I work as a free-lance quantitative and qualitative researcher.

THANKS

I would like to thank Dr George Clegg, whose experience of applied statistics has covered both academia and the defence industry. Having asked a lot of hard questions about what I intended to do, he became the book's first reader. He is the *eminence grise* behind the project.

The main non-statistical reader has been Kerin Freeman, the editor and writer based in New Zealand. I am also very grateful for readings and comments by Elinor Hannay in Australia and Diana Kealey in Manchester. Also, I would like to acknowledge the encouragement at different stages from Iain Buchan of the University of Manchester and StatsDirect, and Ruth Hawthorn of the National Institute of Careers Education and Counselling in London (sorry, I know you wanted a course).

I appreciate their contributions, but remain, of course, responsible for any shortcomings.

TALKING POINT

You do not need mathematics any more than I do to use statistics effectively.

CHAPTER TWO

DESCRIPTIVE STATISTICS INTRODUCED.

The focus of this book is on inferential statistics, where we make generalisations from limited amounts of data. Some knowledge of descriptive statistics is essential, however, for three reasons: it is useful in itself, it is essential preparatory work before using statistical tests, and it provides concepts underlying the use of statistical tests.

Descriptive statistics refer to both quantities and also the *shape* of the data. Before getting involved in this, we need to define the word *statistic*: as a singular noun, a statistic is a number which represents or summarises data.

THE LIMITATIONS OF ABSOLUTE DATA

There are times when you can just say it as it is. We have: 99 red balloons; 20,000 drug addicts; 101 Dalmatians.

Some uncontroversial statistics - figures representing groups of data – can also be used. A common one is the *range*, formed from the maximum and minimum values. When given as a single statistic, this is Max minus Min: so if the highest value is 206 and the lowest value is 186, then the Range statistic would be 20.

Problems emerge, however, when we compare groups of data, or *data sets*. If we look at, for example, the earnings of individuals in countries of different sizes, a direct comparison may be misleading. We therefore tend to use 'averages': the description is then along the lines of the average person earning a lot in this country, and very little in that one, regardless of the comparative sizes.

THE AVERAGE (OR CENTRAL TENDENCY)

Although I am trying to avoid mathematics wherever possible, one particular statistic is a key to understanding statistics as a discipline. Relax, however: almost everyone will have heard of the concept of averages.

An *average* has another title, one which is longer but perhaps more meaningful: it is a measure of *central tendency*. Roughly, it defines the middle of the data being examined.

The word 'average', however, is rather a layman's term when applied to statistics. If a newspaper article claims that the average wage or salary is X pounds/dollars/roubles, what is meant? Let us look at three definitions of central tendency: the mean, the mode and the median.

The *mean* is an average calculated by adding together the numbers involved and then dividing the resulting number by the number of items, as in the simple example of this data set of five numbers: **2, 3, 3, 4, 8**. The sum, $\sum$, $= 2 + 3 + 3 + 4 + 8 = 20$. The number of items, $N = 5$. The mean is, therefore, $\sum / N$: $20/5 = 4$.

The *mode* is the number that comes up most often. In the previous example, this would be the number 3.

When the list is spread, as above, from the biggest to the smallest, then the *median* is the value sitting in the middle of the string of numbers. We count inwards from the string of numbers in our example, discounting first the 2 and the 8, then the outer 3 and the 4, and we are left with the number 3 as the median.

To illustrate the potential use of these measures of central tendency, let us return to the newspaper article referring to 'average' pay. I don't know which statistic any given newspaper is referring to and I suspect that the reader (and possibly the writer) doesn't either. Without making a judgement, however, let us look briefly at the possibilities.

The *mean* takes the wages of all the paid workers in the city, adds them together and divides the total by the number of the workers, as if to see what one worker would have if all were equally paid. The strength of this statistic, that it takes into account the multimillionaire through to the poorest paid, can also be its weakness. Distortions created by, for example, one or two billionaires, could lead to a rather unrepresentative statistic (see the following section for further discussion of this issue). The mean is used a lot within statistical calculations.

The *mode* may deal with this problem: most wage-payers may, for example, be administrative workers and office workers. Their wage will become the average when using the mode, but how informative will this be when trying to describe the earnings of the workforce in general?

The *median* may find a central value, perhaps a middle-manager's salary. This is useful, as are the other statistics, but it may not indicate the most common wage (as the mode would) nor would it take into account to any extent the many people on poor pay and the considerable purchasing power of the very rich.

My reasons for concentrating on the concept of central tendency or the 'average' are both to reflect the importance of the concept and to demonstrate more broadly that data may be subject to different interpretations, of differing degrees of usefulness depending upon the context.

THE DISTRIBUTION OF DATA

Averages are just part of what is known as the distribution of data. Data can be shown in a histogram; we again use our string of numbers: 2, 3, 3, 4, 8.

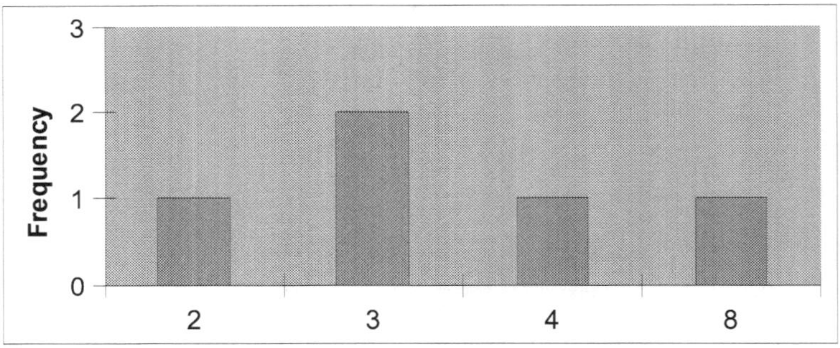

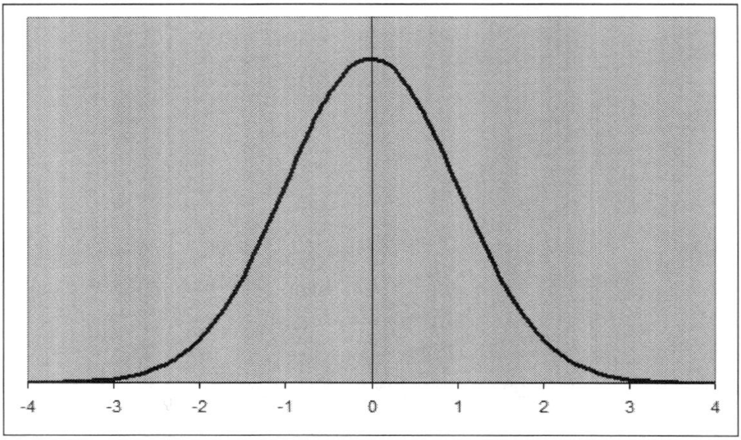

In cases where we have more data – often where the data represents a natural population, for example, using automobile maximum speeds or intelligence test results – we get a distribution. One common type of distribution is the 'normal distribution', the famous bell curve (an idealised symmetrical one is shown below).

If you look up the *Help* file of StatsDirect and look up *Distributions/Normal Distributions*, you will see various shapes which are all normal distributions. There are other types of distribution, for example, binomial, Poisson and even random.

The consistency or otherwise of a distribution is particularly relevant when choosing between parametric and non-parametric tests. The appropriate use of descriptive statistics will be referred to when we look at test usage.

Regardless of whether or not the distribution is normal, various statistics are derived from the distance around the mean. Although these statistics have a considerable effect on calculations made by statistical software and are cited regularly in textbooks on statistics, we need not be overly concerned with them here. What is important is the general concept of *variance*. Variability of data around the mean – movement away from the central tendency - can be the tell-tale effect that we think we are examining or, as will be seen, it can be other factors.

Talking Point

All manner of additional statistics are churned out both by statistical packages and by books on statistics. One example is *kurtosis*, a statistic representing the degree of flatness of the curve surrounding a distribution histogram. The author has never used this in his research and it is unlikely that you will.

Another point: there are times when descriptive statistics are all you need. Inferential statistics should only be used when there is something you want to find out (infer) from the data.

Chapter Three

Inferential Statistics Introduced

Inferring can mean jumping to conclusions. I hope to show that we can logically view some data and come to *reasonable* conclusions about them. In this chapter, I ask the reader to bear with me while learning some key concepts. Soon after this, we are ready to practise using the tests.

Samples from Populations

Generally, we tend to examine collections of data which are *samples* from a wider *population*. 'Population' can have its usual meaning, the total number of people in a town or country, but in research terms, this often means a group of interest to us, or target group. This could be employees or students, or more narrowly, bank clerks or biology students.

As it is usually impractical to observe, question or test a whole population, for example, biology students in the whole of Canada, we usually limit ourselves to *samples* from the target population. Samples could comprise bank clerks from a selection of banks in a small town, or biology students from three colleges in different regions. Given limitations in resources, samples can be even more restricted than this.

Some rules of thumb have been proposed for sample size in terms of being representative of a population (Roscoe, J.T. (1975) *Fundamental research statistics for the behavioral sciences*. New York: Holt, Rinehart and Winston): most research can be appropriately covered by sample sizes of between about 30 and 500, with 500 representing a population of millions. Simple, tightly controlled studies (for example, with matching pairs of participants) can have as few as 10 to 20 participants. The breaking down of samples into subsamples (e.g. males/females, supervisors/workers) requires at least thirty participants per category. Multivariate techniques and also multiple regression require a sample size several times as large as the number of *variables* (variables are discussed in the chapter on the Analysis of Differences), preferably 10 times as many. The author would suggest that relatively small samples may be used for surveys, as long as it is recognised that there are dangers of being rather unrepresentative and also that very real (if small) effects may be missed.

In this book, small samples of data have been chosen, with often fairly artificial characteristics, in order for the reader to enter data quickly.

LOOKING FOR AN EFFECT

If we measure an entire population, what we see is what is out there. Assuming reliable measurement, descriptive statistics would be sufficient for illustrating any perceived phenomenon. Such a phenomenon is the *effect*.

We are never sure, however, about just how representative a sample is of the population from which it is drawn. The reason for using statistical tests, at least at this introductory level, is to find out about the likely existence of an *effect*, or its absence, when using a sample of data. Essentially, we are interested in whether or not there are real differences between two or more sets of data or, in correlational designs, whether or not there are real relationships between them. These are *effects*.

SIGNIFICANCE

For those of you who have previously been introduced to statistics and have been baffled by the 'p values' or 'null hypotheses'/ 'alternative hypotheses', this section is for you! **All readers should read this section carefully.**

It should be noted that I referred to *real* differences or relationships between data. With any samples, we cannot be sure of whether or not an effect is meaningful. The perceived effect could, in fact, be a chance fluctuation in the sample data or the influence of a different and perhaps unexpected effect.

The search for meaningfulness is the point of *significance testing*. Is the perceived phenomenon a fluke or not? Let us say, for example, that the same sample of people have their typing speeds measured on a Monday and on a Tuesday. You want to know if the day of the week matters - *does Monday differ from Tuesday* in terms of employee performance – but, you are also aware that extraneous factors (such as the journey in to work on a given day, or illness) could also affect results. The use of statistics here would be to see if there is a significant difference between the typing speeds on the two days.

Academic texts refer to the *null hypothesis*. The null hypothesis states that any perceived effect is, in fact, a matter of chance or a non-relevant factor. If, in our example, any differences in performance are likely to be down to a cold or a traffic jam, then *the null hypothesis is accepted*. In everyday terms, the result is *not significant*.

If, however, the effect is clear-cut – regardless of a few people having a bad day, there is a clear difference between the performances on Monday and on Tuesday – then, academically speaking, *the null hypothesis is rejected*, or *the alternative hypothesis* (the alternative to chance fluctuation) *is accepted*. In everyday terms, the result is *significant*.

I have mentioned these definitions of hypotheses, as you will encounter them in text books, academic reporting and, sometimes, in statistical software results. When reporting in applied research, however, and for your own sanity, the fluke / chance / interfering factors / null result can be referred to as *not significant*. The 'real' effect can be referred to as a *significant* effect or result.

But why have I discussed these issues in what appears to be the wrong order, starting with the non-significant (null hypothesis) result and only then the sought-after significant result? Essentially, tests of significance are concerned with the likelihood of an effect being the result of extraneous factors. These calculations of variance about the mean, like the computers running them, do not share your enthusiasm for that significant effect; they are seeking out the *probability of a chance result.*

There is a lot of theory about probability, starting from simple branching – heads and tails – through to mind-exploding calculations. All that you need to consider here is the question, 'is the effect significant or a matter of irrelevant fluctuation?'

Which takes us to the '*p value*'. The p value of a test is the measure of significance. It tells us *the likelihood of a result being insignificant!*

The percentage of the p value is the calculated chances of your test result being a fluke. Let us say, for example, that the precise p value is .03. This means that there is a three in a hundred chance that the result has emerged from irrelevant fluctuations. It therefore seems rather likely that your result is significant.

Try not to get carried away, however, by starting to talk about 97% success rates or anything like that. Stick to the .03. What it really means is that, according to the statistical calculations, if you tried the test on a hundred samples, then there is a 3% chance that the data could yield a fluke result. Yes, it looks good, but your result could still be that three-in-a-hundred irrelevance.

A corollary of this is that if you used 100 samples, there is a likelihood that you could end up with three misleading results. There is a practical side to this: if you run a series of tests, a temptation when dealing with a complicated data set, the chance of some of them being fluke results increases considerably. This is why replication of results is often recommended in academic journals and - if the result is at all important to your business - it may well be sensible in practice. (See the example of reliability testing using the Pearson Test within the chapter on correlations.)

A high p value, for example, .337 (the highest number is 1), is very suggestive of a fluke. .333 informs us that there is a one in three chance of your results being due to a random or irrelevant fluctuation. Although you could replicate this, it does not seem worth it. But, what level of significance is worth considering?

Generally, we do not refer to a precise p value. Computers often and researchers almost always, refer to the p value in more general terms: p is smaller than something. Commonly quoted p values are $p < 0.05$, $p < 0.01$ and $p < 0.001$ respectively. The chances of a fluke result are calculated as being less than five in a hundred (5%), less than one in a hundred and less than one in a thousand; $p < .02$ and $p < .005$ are not unheard of. All refer to the likelihood of any variance being a matter of chance or unexpected factors.

Although it is quite common to merely 'read off' the p values from the computerised results, some would argue that the researcher should decide upon an acceptable level of significance *before* using the statistical tests. The point is that there should be an acceptable level of risk (or academic rigour). While $p < .05$ may be acceptable to a psychologist using a sample of twenty students, where it may be difficult to find a significant result and where the experiment can be replicated easily next year, a business may, in some cases, want the chance of an error to be less than $p < .01$. An aircraft manufacturer, however, may want $p < .001$, with replications. In any case, the question is, should the researcher decide on what is acceptable *after* looking at the results?

A final point when deciding upon which level of significance is acceptable is the question of *one-tailed* and *two-tailed* hypotheses. A one-tailed hypothesis means that you know from the start, because of the nature of the exercise, in which direction the effect is going; a two-tailed means that you can not be sure in which direction a significant result would run. (These terms relate to variance from the mean to only one end of the distribution versus possible variance to both sides.) If you were sure, for example, that the typing speeds would be worse on Mondays than on Tuesdays (and this was indeed the result), if the statistical test indicates that $p < .01$, you can accept that there was a less than 1% chance of a fluke result. If, however, you weren't committed to which day was likely to result in faster typing, a chance result was twice as likely and, in the interests of rigour, you should be accepting a two-tailed result: the p value doubles and you accept $p < .02$ two-tailed. (In academic reporting, you would refer to the result being significant at $p < .01$ one-tailed or significant at $p < .02$ two-tailed. In reporting in non-academic reports, you would just quote the level of significance as being smaller than .01 or .02).

TALKING POINT

If you already have the data for a whole population, you don't need to infer: a population is already representative of itself. You may, however, use inferential tests to compare (or contrast) one part of the population with another. They may differ in more ways than just the measure in which you are interested, so the test can allow for fluctuations.

Chapter Four

On The Nature Of Numbers

An important concern in quantitative research is that of *the criterion problem.* The criterion is the subject of measurement. If the criterion, that which is being measured, is inaccurate or inappropriate for the test being used, then no estimations of significance can be considered valid. One has built on a house of cards. Although the accuracy of measurement is more a matter of research design and is therefore not our primary concern in this book, the issue of data being appropriate for test purposes must be discussed.

Different tests carry different assumptions about the data they analyse. Such assumptions become particularly important when deciding whether or not to use parametric tests (to be discussed shortly) and in considering the quantification of qualitative statistics (yes!) later in the book.

The nature of numbers is fundamental to using statistical tests. Running tests with inappropriate data can lead to a mass of apparently significant (or insignificant) results which are, in fact, meaningless. This sort of error is easily made and computer software packages in many cases will not be any more aware of the problem than you are. This is, of course, a good reason for examining data before testing, including using descriptive charts.

You must ensure that the data you input is appropriate. In most cases, this includes using the same type of numbers in all data sets used.

One way of conceptualising the different types of data used is to consider its texture. Is it finely chopped or coarse?

Ratio Interval Ordinal Categorical (Nominal/Qualitative)

-----Continuous-----

Continuous data exists as a run of information which has 'natural' proportions. Distances, seconds and prices (where unbanded) are of this kind. Ratio data runs from zero (e.g., 0, 1 dollar, 2 dollars, 3 dollars…), while interval data can start above zero (as in typing speeds per minute: 30 wpm, 31 wpm, 32 wpm, 33 wpm, etc.). In terms of statistical calculations, there is no difference between ratio and interval types of continuous data. Continuous data is usually the grist for parametric tests.

At times, you may be unsure as to whether or not you are dealing with truly continuous data. Ask yourself if doubling (or halving) a given amount will give a meaningful result. IQ results, for example, appear to be interval data, but are you sure that somebody with an IQ of 140 has exactly twice the measured intelligence as somebody tested as having an IQ of 70? Similarly, the idea of doubling or halving a Likert Scale from a questionnaire (see below) is a dubious one:

1	2	3	4	5	6
Very Unsatisfied	Un-satisfied	In-different	Satisfied	Very Satisfied	Ecstatic

More coarsely grained numbers are usually subsumed within *ordinal numbers*. IQ and most Likert scales truly belong here (unless the latter are very well calibrated, but Item Response Theory is well outside the remit of this book and is not usually come across in everyday questionnaire work). The same would be true of an arbitrary set of prices (£1.40, £2.99), ranges of pay (£15,000-£20,000, £21,000-£30,000) and various other measures which are not strictly continuous.

Ordinal data is so-called because it can be ordered, or ranked. There is a quantitative difference between numbers - one is bigger than another - even if they are not 'smooth' and cannot be arithmetically manipulated like continuous numbers. This sort of data is generally examined by non-parametric tests (see below), which puts them into a rank order of magnitude.

At the far end of our data continuum is *categorical* data, otherwise known as *nominal* or *qualitative* data. My old physics teacher referred to the concept as 'elephants and telegraph poles' when referring to entities which do not mix. I can't remember the precise context, or almost anything else I was taught in physics, but this concept of exclusive differentiation stuck. Categorical data can be *dichotomous* (male/female, or yes/no). It can also include classifications arbitrarily decided by the researcher: examples could include types of employee (manual, clerical, managerial), people holding specific viewpoints (hostile to a concept, approving, indifferent) or even agglomerations of ranges of numbers (well-paid, comfortable, in dire straits).

Each category must be exclusive: each observation is only counted in the *frequency* of one category.

This qualitative choice raises an issue which should be considered throughout your data analysis or research. There needs to be a theory behind your decision-making. I do not mean academic theories (although these may be considered in order to make sense of what you are doing), but some form of rationale. Without this, you may, in effect, be doing something similar to just putting data into the computer and hoping that what emerges is meaningful – which it usually isn't.

(Mixed data, including dichotomous, or binary data, can be subjected to logistic regression, but that takes us outside this introductory volume.)

PARAMETRIC VERSUS NON-PARAMETRIC DATA

In both tests of differences between data sets and also tests involving correlation (relationships between data), the test user will sometimes discover a choice between using parametric and non-parametric tests.

Parametric tests are used when certain *assumptions* are made about the parameters (the limits and nature) of the data. These tests should only be made if the assumptions are met. Data should be continuous, as in being naturally proportioned, should form a recognised distribution, and should contain homogeneity of variance. Essentially, homogeneity of variance means that numbers in the data sets should be of the same proportion (*not*, for example, 2, 3, 4, 5, 3 tested against 23, 28, 33, 46, 30).

As a rule of thumb, experimental and quasi-experimental data (see Analysis of Differences chapter), when continuous, may be suitable candidates for parametric tests. A strict test of data suitability, looking for normal distribution, is provided by StatsDirect: the Shapiro-Wilk test.

If the assumptions are not met but you are still using measurable data (i.e., of different numerical quantities, but not categorical data), then you should use non-parametrics. Non-parametric tests are designed to ignore the lop-sidedness of data. If, for example, we had the numbers 16, 15, 13, 32, 4, 4, 3, a parametric test would certainly be much affected by the far-flung number (assuming that 32 is an outlier rather than an error). A non-parametric test would rank the data:

32 (1st), 16 (2nd), 15 (3rd), 12 (4th), 4 (5th equal), 4 (5th equal), 3 (7th).

As would be usual when using statistical tests, you would check your descriptive statistics first. Is the outlier (32, in this case) a legitimate part of your data set? If it is a matter of poor data entry, one can alter this as appropriate. If you decide that this was an uncharacteristic performance (maybe the respondent had an unfair advantage) you may consider deleting that record (although such a decision should be carefully considered and recorded). If the outlier is legitimate, a non-parametric test can use the data without being unduly influenced by its extreme nature.

TALKING POINT

Many books recommend the use of parametric tests wherever possible. They are considered to be 'more powerful' than their non-parametric alternatives and should, therefore, be able to detect significant results which may otherwise be missed. The choice, however, is most dependent upon conditions. As most data analysis conditions in everyday research are not text-book examples, non-parametric tests are more likely to be used. In any case, when confronted with data suitable for parametric tests, non-parametric tests often produce very similar results.

Chapter Five

Data Analysis in Practice

Here, we make our first reference to using StatsDirect.

When practising, people find different ways of approaching problems. What is suggested below is just one way of structuring your work.

Decide What it is You Want to Measure First - Have a Rationale

Ideally, you will have designed the data collation yourself, thus meeting your knowledge needs and making it easy to analyse. Often, however, you are given the data and it is left to you to analyse it. In either case, you need to decide what you want to discriminate between, categorise or compare. As I hope will be quite clear, just inputting data and hoping the 'results' are significant is likely to mislead you and everybody else.

Look at the Descriptive Statistics

StatsDirect breaks this into two, descriptive statistics (numeric) and graphics (pictorial).

Open the 'Test' worksheet in StatsDirect (if it isn't already open, use File/Open File/Test). Select two or three data sets and then use Analysis/Descriptive/Univariate Summary. You will generally want to report the means for your data sets. Large differences between the means often indicate differences between data sets.

Then use Graphics to look at your data. Box & Whisker charts are useful for analysis of differences: in significantly different data sets, these will tend to diverge. The Box & Whisker contains a set of the statistics we have already described. The 'whiskers' at each end represent the Minimum and Maximum values and the bar with a diamond represents the Median. The 'box' is based on the quartile system, which extends the 'median' idea of the central spread of the data: the box represents central data, but unlike the median, it covers half of all of the total data for the variable.

Chart Maker or Scatter are useful for examining potential correlations.

DECIDE ON THE TEST TO BE USED

These issues will be described in more detail in the rest of the book. For deciding if parametric tests are applicable for a data set, however, use Analysis / Parametric/Shapiro-Wilk, a test for examining normal distribution.

RECORD, EXPAND AND REPORT

Decisions made, including the omission of data, should be recorded. Raw data and cross-tabulations may be transferred to Microsoft Excel for the creation of additional charts. Reporting of data is discussed later in the book.

TALKING POINT

As will become obvious later, it is important to examine data in a graphical format before getting carried away with the wildly significant (or depressingly insignificant) results of your statistical test.

Section TWO:

Statistical Testing

Chapter Six

The Analysis Of Differences

Deciding on the Question

People thinking about everyday data may think of research design as a rather abstract concept. Design needs to be considered, however, every time we ponder which question should be asked (if any). The question of design must be posed before an appropriate test can be selected. It is presumed here, however, that we have already decided that we want to test for significant differences between data sets.

Unrelated Versus Related Design

On each occasion, we need to look at the constituents of the sample.

In *unrelated design*, different participants/records are used in each condition. If we are testing for differences between typing speeds on Mondays and Tuesdays, this would mean one group of staff being tested on a Monday, and a different group of staff being tested on a Tuesday. Although this would get rid of order effects (e.g., people getting bored with tests on the second occasion) or practice effects (getting better with practice), there is an obvious problem: any test is going to have to take into account a range of individual differences and is going to differ from a test applied to related designs.

Related design endeavours to get rid of these individual differences by one of two methods. The *same* people can be used in all conditions; in our typing example, the same people are tested on both Monday and Tuesday. This eliminates individual differences entirely, although not order/practice effects or the possibility of having a 'bad day'.

Another related design method is the *pairing (or matching)* of different participants for particular characteristics. In our typing example, although different people are tested on each day, each person's results are paired with the results of another person with, say, the same pre-tested typing speed, maybe also controlled for gender and seniority. This being the case, we eliminate practice/ order effects while also eliminating some individual differences. In terms of testing, the paired or matched design is usually subsumed under the related design category.

Here are some alternative terms you may come across:

Unrelated Design	*Related Design*
Different subjects/participants	Same subjects/participants
Between-subjects Design	Within-subjects Design
Unpaired	Paired
Unmatched	Matched
	Repeated Measures (the same over time)
	Panel Data (the same people over time, but this term is used in business statistics/econometrics)

TWO OR MORE CONDITIONS

Our discussion of Monday and Tuesday dealt with two conditions. Another example of a two condition test would be the comparison of 'before and after' treatment (e.g., pre-operation, post-operation). In our typing example, however, we may wish to extend our analysis to every day of the week (giving five *conditions*). Another example would examine the differences between a range of different medical treatments (T1, T2, T3).

DATA TYPE

This section deals with quantitative data, where, at the very least, each observation can be compared numerically. For nominal (categorical) data, see the chapter on Qualitative Research.

A NOTE ON RESEARCH DESIGN TERMINOLOGY

In our typing example, we are running an *experiment* (even if not strictly controlled under laboratory conditions). We are manipulating *variables*, types of phenomena which are changeable (variable). We are actively manipulating an *independent variable*; in the typing example, we are interested in the effect of the day of the week; it could be, however, the type of medical treatment, or a single treatment effect. We observe the effect of manipulating the independent variable by looking at changes in the *dependent variable,* that which is being measured. The dependent variable can be typing speeds, time of recovery from illness, the number of relapses, etc. The independent variable is varied according to the will of the experimenter, independent of real life if you like, with the dependent variable being the data dependent on such variations. The terms independent variable and dependent variable should, strictly speaking, only be used in relation to experimental data but are widely used by some writers in other contexts.

Most 'real world' analyses of differences between data sets are *quasi-experimental*. We do not manipulate variables ourselves but take them from records or from observations without planned allocation of participants into groups; and, if we choose to use pairing/matching (comparing people with similar relevant attributes), this would be done through taking details from records rather than actually selecting groups of people for an experiment. In a quasi-experimental version of our typing speeds study, the effect of the day of the week would be called a *predictor* (rather than an independent variable) and the typing speed would be the *criterion* (rather than the dependent variable).

The *predictor* and the *criterion* are a similar pair of terms, which should be used in non-experimental research, although these are often interchangeable with independent and dependent variables in the literature. Both terms are used in the following example (ignore the results: we would, of course, want more than 5 records in each condition).

Independent Variable / Predictor: Day of the Week

	Condition 1: Monday	**Condition** 2: Tuesday
Dependent	40	50
Variable /	30	40
Criterion:	45	45
Typing speed	60	50
(in wpm)	45	43

Because this book is largely about non-experimental situations, the predictor/criterion terminology will be used throughout the rest of the book.

And now, to the tests!

Same Subjects, Two Conditions

Wilcoxon – A Non-Parametric Test

In this example, the same customers have filled in a 5-point scale describing their attitudes toward a company's milk chocolate and also that of a rival company. Lower scores indicate hostility, higher scores approval. As this scale has not undergone preliminary calibration, a non-parametric test has been chosen. Being a small data set, we settled for a .05 level of significance; but as we did not know which product would be preferred, we opted for the more rigorous two-tailed hypothesis.

		Predictor: Milk Chocolate Product	
		Condition 1: Ours	**Condition** 2: Theirs
Criterion:	person 1	4	5
Attitude	person 2	3	3
	person 3	2	4
	person 4	4	5
	person 5	3	5
	person 6	4	2
	person 7	3	3
	person 8	5	4
	person 9	3	5
	person 10	4	5
	person 11	3	5
	person 12	2	4
	person 13	2	5

Open File/New Workbook and then enter the numbers given again, with 'Ours' and 'Theirs' at the top of each column of numbers. As you will use this data again and add to it, save the file (File/Save) and give it a name (e.g., choc.sdw).

For those not familiar with manipulating data, data in more than one non-adjacent column can be selected by holding down the Control (Ctrl) button during selection.

If we look at our descriptive data (Analysis/Descriptive/ Univariate Summary), we will see a difference of 1 between the means, quite a lot when considering a five point scale used by only 13 people, and a different median. Select Graphics/Box & Whisker to view the differences between the data.

We want to ascertain, however, that the more positive result for 'Theirs' is significant, so we use the Wilcoxon test. We use Analysis/Non-Parametric/Wilcoxon. If we had been considering a one-tailed test of significance, the p value would have been .021: $p < .05$. The two-tailed test (StatsDirect uses the term two-sided), however, gives a value of .042, still $p < .05$. We can report the difference as being significant, $p < .05$ two-tailed.

Paired t-test (also known as Related t-test) – a Parametric Test

Students who didn't pass an examination initially, all achieving less than the 40 point pass mark, retake their examinations with generally improved results ('First'). They retake a second time ('Second') in an attempt to improve their grades.

		Predictor: Examination Retakes	
		Condition 1: First	**Condition** 2: Second
Criterion:	**person 1**	52	60
Score	person 2	53	34
	person 3	47	38
	person 4	40	52
	person 5	48	54
	person 6	45	55
	person 7	52	36
	person 8	47	48
	person 9	51	44
	person 10	38	56

Again, it is suggested that you save the input of these numbers (e.g., retake1), as you will add to the data shortly. Check that the data can be considered to have a normal distribution. This is confirmed by using Analysis/Parametric/Shapiro-Wilk. Then check the descriptive and graphical information: there is an increase in the mean score (0.4) and an increase in the median, but the Box and Whisker plot looks ambiguous.

We now use Analysis/Parametric/Paired t. The large p values tell us that the difference is not significant.

Same Subjects, More Than Two Conditions

Friedman – A Non-Parametric Test

This extends the Wilcoxon test. We use it here to expand on our work with both our examples from the Wilcoxon test and from the Paired t-test.

		Predictor: Milk Chocolate Product		
		Condition 1: Ours	**Condition** 2: Theirs	**Condition** 3: Ours Adapted
Criterion:	person 1	4	5	5
Attitude	person 2	3	3	3
	person 3	2	4	2
	person 4	4	5	2
	person 5	3	5	2
	person 6	4	2	2
	person 7	3	3	1
	person 8	5	4	3
	person 9	3	5	2
	person 10	4	5	4
	person 11	3	5	2
	person 12	2	4	3
	person13	2	5	1

Re-opening the file containing survey reactions to our chocolate products, add the column of figures in the third column (the other columns are unchanged). Our company, worried by the onslaught of the rival product, has produced a new improved variety.

Use the mouse to select all three columns and use Analysis/ Non-Parametric/Friedman. The initial screen gives a p value of .0003 ($p < .001$), a highly significant result.

Now, using the 'Multiple Comparisons' option, press Calculate. As before, the relationship between the first two conditions is significant at the level of p < .05 (the approximate p value here being .02). There are also significant differences between 'Ours Adapted' and both of the other conditions.

A glance at the means in the descriptive data indicates that this new product is perceived as being worse than its predecessor as well as the rival product. We can also check to see if this trend is significant, using the Cuzick Trend test (under Non-Parametrics). If you don't want to bother with specifying group scores (SUM from the descriptive data) during this process, it is suggested that you copy the columns in the workbook in the following order (following the trend) - 'Ours Adapted', 'Ours', 'Theirs' – and then use the Cuzick test. Oh dear! The trend is highly significant: back to the drawing board.

Predictor: Examination Retakes

Condition 1:	**Condition** 2:	**Condition** 3:
First	Second	Third

Re-opening the file containing retake examination results, enter the following ten numbers alongside the other two columns of data.

62, 56, 40, 37, 62, 56, 68, 55, 68, 60.

Our candidates have tried again and we are back using the Friedman test. The initial screen gives a p value of .0156 (p < .02). Something is significant there.

Now, using the 'Multiple Comparisons' option, press Calculate. As before, the relationship between the first two conditions is not significant, but there are significant differences between the scores from the third retake when compared with either of the preceding scores. This does not tell us the reason, however; perhaps some other effect is in play.

TALKING POINT

It is a commonplace truism that correlations (to be discussed later in this volume) do not prove 'cause and effect'. As the above example suggests, however, neither do quasi-experimental structures.

Different Subjects, Two Conditions

Mann-Whitney – A Non-Parametric Test

A chain of estate agents regularly receives complaints about the endowment policies it recommends for the paying-off of mortgages. It is now examining the effects of different types of warning notice upon the level of complaints made about each office. Some offices have a wall-poster describing the situations in which endowments are appropriate for mortgages, others pass their clients leaflets as part of a sales pack.

	Predictor: Warning Method			
	Condition 1: Wall-Poster		**Condition** 2: Leaflet	
Criterion:	office 1	5	office 11	6
Number of complaints (per branch)	office 2	4	office 12	15
	office 3	16	office 13	4
	office 4	6	office 14	4
	office 5	7	office 15	6
	office 6	22	office 16	7
	office 7	8	office 17	16
	office 8	9	office 18	7
	office 9	9	office 19	5
	office 10	8	office 20	4

In each condition, we are told by the Shapiro-Wilk test that 'the sample is unlikely to be from a normal distribution', so we should be using a non-parametric test. After checking descriptives, we use the Mann-Whitney test to find out if the differences between the means are significant. Use Analysis/Non-Parametric/Mann-Whitney and find large p values: there is no significant difference between the data sets and, therefore, no significant difference between the use of wall-posters and of leaflets in this scenario. It is suggested that you save this data set (e.g., 'mortgage').

Unpaired t-test (Also Known as Independent t-test) – A Parametric Test

In research into the effects of different office conditions, one group of office workers is given a lengthy proof-reading task to do within enclosed offices; the other group does the same task in an open-plan office.

	Predictor: Office Conditions			
	Condition 1: Own Office		**Condition** 2: Open Plan	
Criterion: Task score	person 1	80	person 15	56
	person 2	68	person 16	69
	person 3	77	person 17	73
	person 4	78	person 18	70
	person 5	85	person 19	61
	person 6	82	person 20	65
	person 7	79	person 21	59
	person 8	76	person 22	60
	person 9	77	person 23	53
	person 10	83	person 24	61
	person 11	84	person 25	62
	person 12	82	person 26	71
	person 13	81		
	person 14	80		

(Notice that in this study, there are different numbers of participants in the different conditions; only 'same subject' studies are required to have the same numbers.)

Each piece of data appears to be normal, using the Shapiro-Wilk test, so we can use a parametric test. The descriptive statistics show different means and we use Analysis/Parametric/Unpaired to use the t-test, which shows a very high significance level. According to this (fictional) data, being in an open plan office seriously impairs performance on a proof-reading task. Please save this file ('office').

Different Subjects, More Than Two Conditions

Kruskal-Wallis – A Non Parametric Test

If we open the file with data on mortgages, previously used with the Mann-Whitney, we can add some data to another column: 8, 4, 3, 12, 4, 4, 9, 8, 32, 6.

This data represents complaints following the use of yet another method of warning, incorporating the necessary warnings into the sales talk. We use Analysis/Non-Parametric/Kruskal-Wallis which can be considered an extension of the Mann-Whitney test. The large p value indicates an insignificant result. Again, there is no significant difference between warning methods. This suffices. The use of 'calculate' to examine individual relationships in this situation (also known as 'dredging') can uncover apparently 'near-significant' data, which can mislead: 'hunting' for tenuous results is likely to multiply (or inflate, if you like) the probability of chance results.

One-Way ANOVA – A Parametric Test

If we open the file about office conditions, we can put the following 16 numbers into a third column: 70, 70, 73, 80, 81, 75, 75, 73, 81, 76, 75, 75, 73, 71, 72, 67.

Although there is a clear productivity advantage in everybody having their own offices, this is expensive. If we were to introduce cubicles to break up the open plan office, would this produce better results than open plan? The new figures represent (fictional) test scores from workers using cubicles.

To examine our three conditions – open plan, enclosed offices, cubicles, use:

Analysis/Analysis of Variance/One Way

The higher the number for the F ratio in the results, the higher the variance: the variable under examination contributes to the overall effect, as opposed to the effect being caused by unknown variables ('error'). A large F ratio, 36.86, gives a high significance level. So far, so good, but what about the relationships between one of our variables and another? We can look at a multiple comparison option (e.g., Tukey), where we see that all three relationships are significant, although one suspects that the effect is less between Own Office and Cubicles, which would be unsurprising, given the nature of the compromise. How about a trend test? If we look at the means (use Descriptive/Univariate Summary), we will find means of 79.42 for Own Office scores, 63.33 for Open Plan and 74.19 for Cubicles. It looks like Cubicles is a sensible compromise between the two other office systems, but is the trend significant? For ease of testing, put the columns in order of magnitude (e.g., Own Office, Cubicles and Open Plan) and then run Analysis/Non-Parametric/Cuzick Trend Test. As we have aligned the columns in order, we can save ourselves time and opt for 'No' when asked to 'specify group scores' (group scores are 'sum' in the descriptive statistics). Cuzick demonstrates a significant trend with little room for doubt.

This table of tests of difference is not exhaustive, but refers to tests used in this chapter.
n.b. *Non-parametric tests can be used with 'parametric' data.*

Test	Design	Conditions	Data
Wilcoxon Paired t-test Friedman	**Same or Paired Subjects**	2 2 3 or more	Non-parametric Parametric Non-parametric
Mann-Whitney Unpaired t-test Kruskal-Wallis 1-way ANOVA	**Different subjects**	2 2 3 or more 3 or more	Non-parametric Parametric Non-parametric Parametric
Cuzick Trend	Flexible – tests for **trend**	3 or more	Non-parametric
Shapiro-Wilk	Diagnostic – tests for normal **distribution**	1 at a time	Any data, to see if suitable for parametric tests

Chapter Seven

Qualitative Research

There will be many occasions on which you may have gathered a lot of information but it does not appear to be quantifiable. People hold different impressions of a government policy; consumers fall into different 'types' of buyers or social class; different categories of situation or behaviour emerge from incident records. The data is nominal: such phenomena may not be assigned numerical values, as membership of one such *category* is not necessarily 'better' or weightier than another. We can count the *frequency* of their occurrence, however.

The statistical analyses here are concerned with comparing what is observed with what may be predicted. If our predictions are founded on chance, what may happen at random, then we are interested in whether or not actual observations differ significantly from predicted observations.

It should be noted, however, that in order to do this accurately, data must be both *exclusive and exhaustive*: all observations from a sample must be allocated to a category in the analysis and each observation can only be allocated to one category.

Dichotomies – the Sign Test

Let us select a case of a simple 'heads or tails' (dichotomous) event. People walk through a park and they can choose to fork left around a clump of trees or they can fork right around the same clump. Assume that the view is pretty much the same in either direction and that the clump looks rather uninviting. If we observe 30 individuals and find that 17 go left and 13 go right, it is likely that any statistical test is likely to find the difference between the observed 17:13 and the predicted 15:15 to be insignificant. (N.b., in the case of a bigger difference, where something significant *might* be happening but you had no way of knowing beforehand in which direction it would happen, then the more rigorous two-tailed level of significance would be preferred to one-tailed.)

If one seeks a comparison with the parameters of the tests for difference, then dichotomous tests are looking at the significance of differences between two conditions within one (within-subjects) variable. Condition 1 is 'Yes' or 'Heads' or 'Left'; Condition Two is 'No' or 'Tails' or 'Right'. Each condition only contains one number, the *frequency*, the number of times each condition has been observed.

Let us take our example with 30 people finding their way past the clump in the tree. Open Analysis/Exact Tests on Counts/Sign. Firstly, enter 30 as the total observation. As a matter of interest, enter 15 – in other words, a 'fifty-fifty' scenario: $p > 0.9999$ is, of course, $p = 1$, which would be predicted as the random scenario. Now we try our 17:13 scenario; leaving 30 in the sample box, enter 17. $P = 0.58$, still insignificant (we select a two-tailed significance level because, even had there been a significant result, we had no reason to expect the direction of the effect to be right rather than left or vice-versa). Again, out of interest, enter 13 in the box instead of 17; the result is the same, as in a single sample, both results are the two sides of the same coin.

Another example of the Sign test:

Would you consider buying X product?
Yes: 63 / 100 No: the rest.

P <.02 two-tailed (compare this to the statistic given in the Sign test). If we had been sure that the product was superior beforehand, we could have used the one-tailed level of analysis: if we had been looking for p < .01 (only a one-in-a-hundred possibility of being chance), then this would have been satisfied.

More Than Two Conditions – the Chi Square Goodness of Fit Test

In the case of 40 people being observed turning left or right at the end of a supermarket aisle, we may expect product placement to influence the outcome. Let us say that the difference is 26:14 and we believe that an organised promotion is working well for one side, against a random shelf arrangement on the other. Then the Sign test would tell us whether or not 26:14 is significantly different from chance. (Because we already have a good idea of the direction of the effect, the one-tailed level of significance would be acceptable.)

As it might be more realistic to bring in 'straight ahead' as a direction, let us extend our analysis to three conditions. (A methodological point: yes, I know some people may reverse back up the aisle and I could have four conditions, but the relatively small numbers, with all too clear a difference in the frequency count, would distort the test. It is perfectly valid to exclude these observations as long as the rationale is clear and the decision is recorded for future scrutiny. It would not be valid, however, if I just did it to 'get significance'.) Let us have a bigger sample:

Left	*Right*	*Forward*
77	66	47

(Total: 190) On the worksheet, put the three numbers in a column. Select: Analysis/Non-parametric/Chi-Square Goodness of Fit and select 'Grouped Frequencies'. The expected frequencies of 63.33 per category represent the total of 190 divided by the 3 conditions (there are times when you might change the 'expected' frequencies, for example, in studies involving genetics, but for the purposes of this study, let us not go there). There are significant differences: $p < .05$

Another example would be a poll of 105 people asking which social ill is the *worst* (note that this is exclusive). Crime = 35; Global warming = 37; Immigration = 33. (We could have had a fourth or fifth: Insurance companies? Advertising?) The expected frequency is 35 per category (105/3) and as suggested by the closeness of all the categories to the expected frequency, any difference is insignificant; $p = 0.892$ The good citizens will be bolting their doors and calling for tougher immigration legislation as the fresh water diminishes and the tides rise…

The Relationship Between Variables – the Chi Square Test of Association

These tests - found within Analysis/Chi-Square Tests – allow a test of the relationship between variables. As well as the points about nominal data and exclusivity mentioned previously, it should also be noted that there should be at least 20 observations in the sample, with at least 5 in each category.

Let us extend our supermarket example: we may want to find out if gender interacts with the nature of the goods on offer - or perhaps men and women have a tendency to walk in different directions?

	Males	Females
Left	40	37
Right	31	35
Forward	25	22

Use the 2 by <u>k</u> option (without trend)

$p = .7673$; non-significant

Another example for examining the significance or otherwise of the *interaction* between variables is that of a product's advertising profile and an intention to buy that product. Here, we can use the 2 by 2 option.

		Have you seen the advertisement?	
		Yes	**No**
	Yes	18	12
Do you intend to buy the product?	**No**	12	30

If we have been prepared to accept $p < .02$, then $p = .0153$ is a significant result. As the results show, there are clear differences between the observed results (above) and the expected results calculated by the statistical method.

The r by c option can be used from worksheet or from input data to use a wider range of variables. It should be noted, however, that in spite of the advantages of being able to look for differences between observed and predicted values (the bigger difference, the better), larger groupings of variables are likely to be less and less meaningful when it comes to interpretation.

TALKING POINT

There are times when data is 'unquantifiable'. When the data is unreliable, no degree of mathematical sophistication can fail to be undermined. Similarly, if there is no way of establishing a sensible 'starting point' or rationale for analysis, then quantification is pointless.

I would merely point out, however, that there are times when those who declare a topic to be immeasurable may be arguing from a viewpoint of personal preference rather than methodological certainty.

Let me take their side for a while, however. A hermeneutic approach is applied to an interview. That interview may give insights into what may lie behind wads of data. It may also be important to find out if such a viewpoint is shared - returning eventually to quantification in order to demonstrate this - and as a starting point for empirical investigations in new directions.

Without a qualitative focus, how could one decide upon which of hundreds of thousands of potential experiments are worth conducting? Essentially, there should be a relationship between statistical work and an interpretative focus. Should these be divorced, however?

This test table refers to *frequencies of observations* within *categories* of a sample.

Number of Variables	Number of Conditions	Focus	Test
One	2 (dichotomy)	Differences	Sign Test
One	More than 2	Difference	Chi Square Goodness of Fit (differences)
Multi-variable	2 or more	Interaction between variables	Chi Square Test of Association

Chapter Eight

Correlations, Regression and Exploratory Factor Analysis

Correlation

Returning to data with measurable differences, we may wish to examine the relationship between one variable and another, its *correlation*. A correlation is summarised by a statistic known as the *correlation coefficient*. This statistic runs from +1 (a perfect positive correlation), through 0 (completely random) to –1 (a perfect negative relationship). The following numbers and scatter plots will illustrate these.

1	1
2	2
3	3
4	4
5	5
6	6

These two columns of numbers are exactly the same. For example: the same people scoring the same on a measure on two occasions. This can be represented visually using a *scatter plot* from the Excel Chart Wizard or via StatsDirect. To use StatsDirect, select Graphics/ Scatter. As we are only looking at one relationship, opt for just one 'series'.

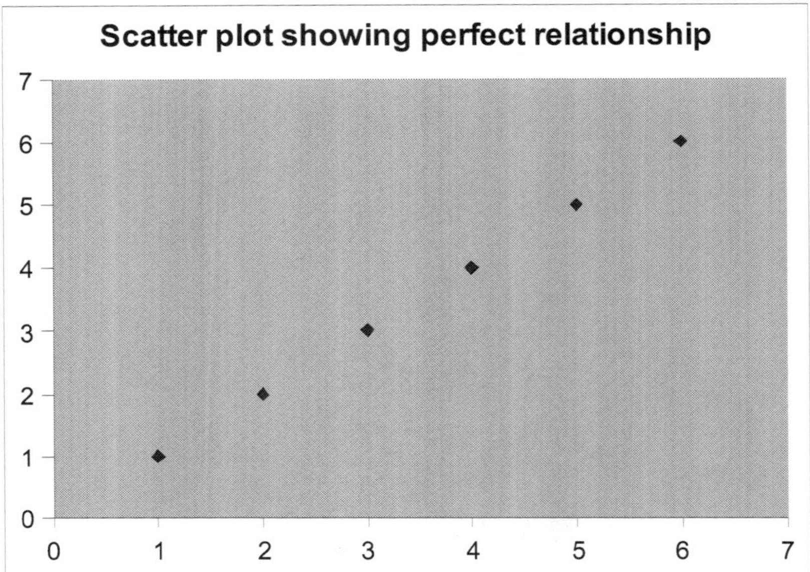

Although one would not expect a perfect relationship in the course of research, a similar slope of this type would indicate a positive relationship between two variables.

1	6
2	5
3	4
4	3
5	2
6	1

Now we juxtapose the inverse, a negative relationship; the higher the score on one of the measures, the lower the score on the other one. This is a perfect *negative* relationship.

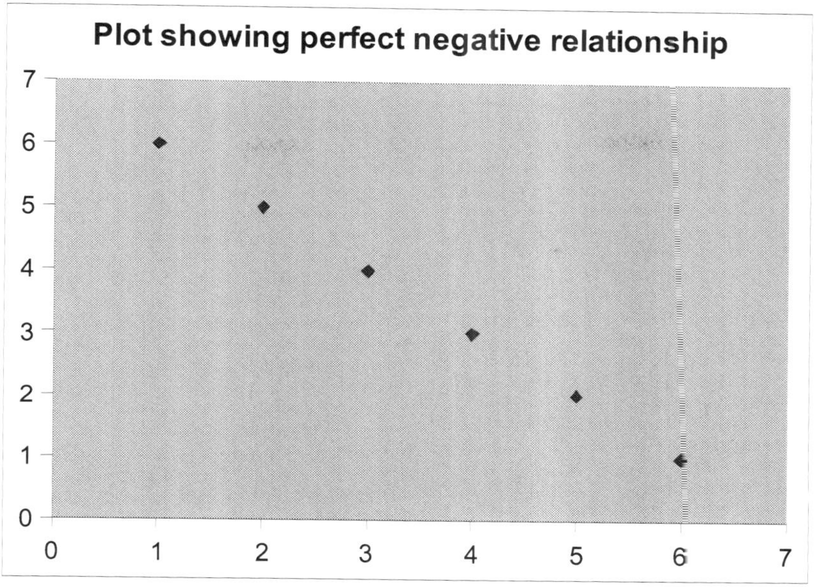

Again, a similar slope, this time rising from right to left, would be indicative of a negative relationship between two variables.

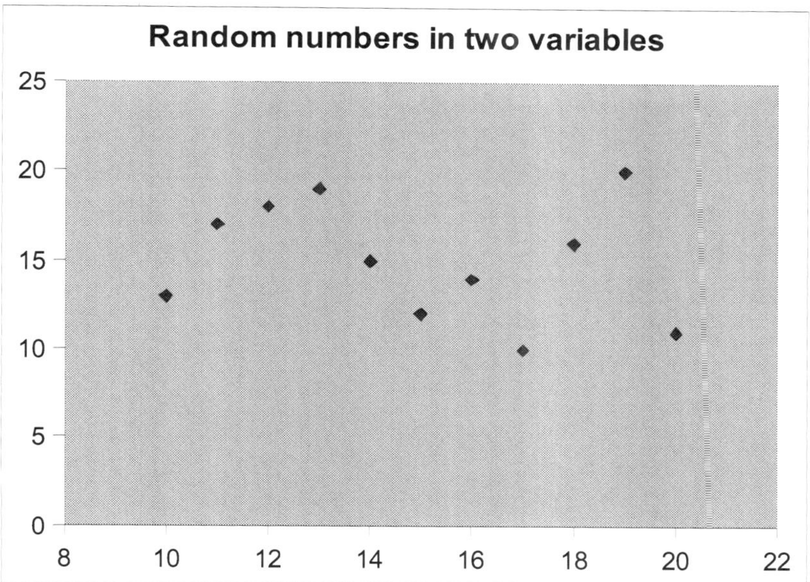

No sensible line could go through this set of relationships. The numbers here were randomly generated. With more numbers involved, a globular cluster is quite typical.

The random numbers used were:

61	16
29	90
22	18
41	10
73	31
36	86
80	65
38	99
49	19
0	57

Now let us use one of the tests.

Two Conditions Tested for a Relationship (Correlation) – Spearman, a Non-Parametric Test

As discussed previously, a non-parametric test does not concern itself overmuch about the nature of the data. This is just as well here, as we are firstly going to ask it about the perfect positive relationship, the perfect negative one and the pair of variables with random scores. Select Analysis/Non-parametric/ Spearman Rank Correlation. (Also reachable by Analysis/ Regression & Correlation/Spearman Rank Correlation.)

On each occasion, choose one of the sets of numbers given above. In the case of the positive perfect relationship, the coefficient (Rho in the case of this test) = 1.

The negative perfect relationship has Rho = -1. Our randomly drawn numbers give a coefficient of 0.2 (i.e., pretty close to zero).

There is a continuum of correlation coefficients:

1 (perfect positive) - - - - - - - - **0** (random) - - - - - **–1** (perfect negative)

Now, let us approach real life. In a survey, people may express confidence in the government, running from very high at rating 1 to very low at rating 5. They may also be rated in terms of confidence in the future, from not confident at 1 to very confident at rating 5.

The scale 'Confidence in the Government' (suggesting that this is at low ebb) is:

5, 1, 2, 4, 4, 3, 5, 5, 3, 4

The scale 'Confidence in the Future' (here, people seem unsure) is:

5, 4, 5, 3, 1, 2, 4, 3, 2, 2

Having seen a fairly bitty scatter plot chart, the Spearman test coefficient turns out to be .06, obviously small. The p level is 0.89; any effect is clearly a matter of chance.

Keep the 'Confidence in the Future' ratings and compare them with the following salaries for each person (in thousands): 28, 30, 25, 27, 18, 20, 15, 24, 18, 22;

assuming that the researcher had predicted beforehand that salary would be positively associated with confidence in the future and that given the small numbers, $p < .05$ was an acceptable level (5 in 100 chance of a fluke finding), then such findings could be accepted at a one-tailed level of analysis ($p < .05$ one-tailed but is greater than that at the two-tailed level).

Did you check the scatter graph for this example? A slope can be discerned.

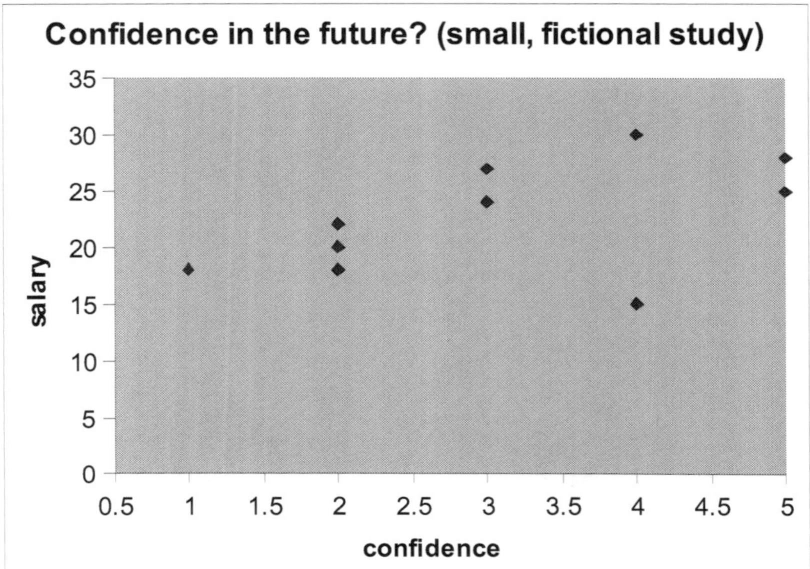

A cautionary note: Why do I insist upon looking at scatter plots in addition to using a test? The reason is that the correlational tests here (non-parametric and parametric) are *linear*. They assume a relationship that runs in one direction, whether positive or negative. If you run a test without looking at a scatter plot as well, there is the danger of assuming significance or lack of it from test results which are really fictitious. Below are two examples of non-linear correlations. One is a real-life error by the author. I examined a friend's blood pressure readings against time (thanks, you know who, for allowing me to reproduce this evidence of my impulsive nature). The coefficient was –0.16, with a two-tailed p level of .3 – a surprise to both of us as we had expected some sort of pattern to emerge. Then, I remembered…

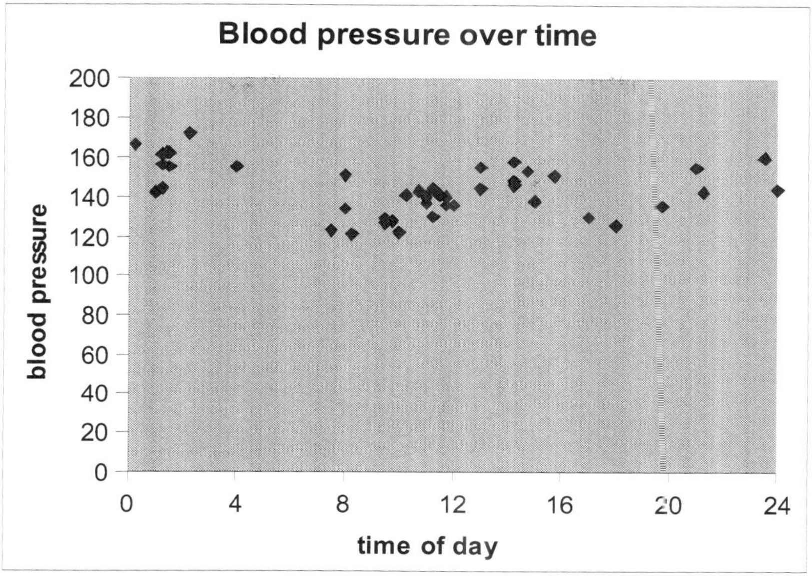

As is suggested by the graph's wave-like formation, there is a tendency towards higher blood pressure readings in the early afternoon and also at night. So there is an effect, but it is not a linear one. While the graph is informative, I should not have used a linear test; the correlations were of course meaningless.

Another non-linear example may be familiar to students of stress and sports fans.

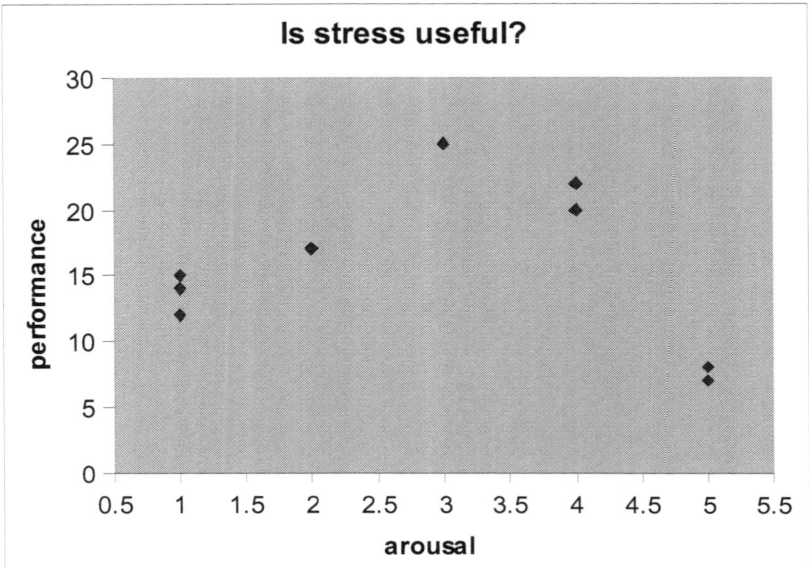

This (fictional) grading of performance against high and low graded stress levels is indicative of what is known as the Yerkes-Dodson Law. Although high stress may damage performance, some degree of stimulation is seen as necessary. Again, this non-linear effect would emerge from a graph but could be erroneously seen as either significant or otherwise if subjected to Spearman's test or a parametric alternative. Essentially, 'curvilinear' relationships should not be subjected to these tests.

Two Conditions Tested for a Relationship (Correlated) – Pearson, a Parametric Test

For this statistical test, select Analysis/Regression & Correlation/Simple Linear Regression & Correlation. As will be seen when we look at regression analysis, there is a close relationship between the two methods. For the moment, however, we are just interested in correlations; Pearson's Product Moment

Correlation provides the correlation coefficient – *r* - required here.

If you reopen the examination retakes file, you should find the following numbers in the third column: 62, 56, 40, 37, 62, 56, 68, 55, 68, 60. If you remember, this represented a significant improvement in examination scores. Suppose now there was the thought that this result may have been a lucky accident: we want to test *reliability* (whether or not a measure is consistent over time). As 'test-retest', however, would be inappropriate because of practice effects, we use a parallel test, which asks different questions about the same taught material.

The new scores are: 65, 55, 39, 43, 66, 54, 73, 58, 72, 64. If we use the scatter plot to examine the relationship between these two variables, we see a positive slope. When you again select Analysis/Regression & Correlation/Simple Linear Regression & Correlation, StatsDirect asks you to 'select data for outcome' and 'select data for predictor': these are important for regression, to be covered shortly, but if we are just using this test for correlation purposes, it does not matter which way round the variables go. The correlation coefficient *r* is .9871, showing a very high significance level; clearly, the examination methodology demonstrates high reliability. (Note also, for the next section, that a statistic called r^2 ['R Squared'] is .97436.)

For an example of a non-significant result using Pearson's correlation, try comparing the first two variables in the examination retake file (data repeated here):

52, 53, 47, 40, 48, 45, 52, 47, 51, 38 __ 60, 34, 38, 52, 54, 55, 36, 48, 44, 56

EFFECT SIZE

Another statistic is worth considering at this stage. Note that when we looked at the significant relationship, r^2 was cited as

= .97436. If you use Tools/Calculator, you will, of course, note that this is indeed the square of the correlation, .9871*.9871 Some people mistake the correlation coefficient (here *r*) as a measurement of the size of the relationship; it is, in fact, an assessment as to whether or not an effect is 'real' (i.e., significant) as opposed to an irrelevant mixture of variables. It is the *effect size* (here r^2) which shows how far the effect accounts for the *variance*, the swing away from the mean.

In the current example, .974 rather than .987 seems of little import, but what about a case where the coefficient *r* is (a still quite high) .63? Here, the effect r^2 .3969 contributes no more than 40% of the variance. Quite often, therefore, a significant result can represent a negligible effect size; .33, for example, gives only 11% of the variance. Cohen (1988) suggests the following categories for effect size (***d***):

0.2 to 0.5 = small effect size; 0.5 to 0.8 = medium; > 0.8 = large.

Various ideas emerge from this. If the rest of the variance is random 'noise', could the research model be improved, made more reliable? Is there another factor at play which could contribute to our understanding of the effect? Is the significant result meaningful in real-world terms, and should we invest in it? These questions become less academic when we look at multiple regression and correlation (MRC).

As a building block, however, we first need to consider regression as a concept.

LINEAR REGRESSION (TWO CONDITIONS)

When we looked at the scatter plot charts for significant relationships between two sets of data, a slope could be ascertained, representing the relationship. A line can be drawn through the incline (assuming it makes sense when considering the real world context), taking us into the realms of prediction. By looking for where the X variable meets the intercept (the line), we can see what value is expected from the Y variable.

NON-PARAMETRIC LINEAR REGRESSION

Use when the data is rather rough-hewn.

Taking a simple (fictional) example, ratings for some individuals with debt-related problems (high ratings indicate worse problems) - 1, 1, 1, 2, 2, 2, 3, 3, 3, 4, 4, 4, 5, 5, 5 - and the rated likelihood of their looking for help (5 meaning they have declared themselves certain to seek help): 3, 1, 1, 2, 1, 2, 3, 2, 3, 2, 3, 4, 4, 5, 5 Select Analysis/Regression & Correlation/ Non-Parametric Linear Regression; use the seeking help ratings as Outcomes and debt levels as Predictors: i.e., will debt levels be a useful guide to the likely take-up of counselling services?

Looking at the intercept, one can see that people with greater problems are likely to seek help, but also that this is by no means certain at an intermediate level; perhaps information about services needs to reach the intermediate problem group before they get into further trouble…

SIMPLE LINEAR REGRESSION (PARAMETRIC LINEAR REGRESSION)

Another example of regression can be found on the commercial data set below. For the moment, let us just look at Sales and Price. Is there a meaningful relationship between these variables, and can we make predictions about how well a product will sell if we change the price? (Before anybody blames me for their financial demise, these are fictional figures. 'Pile High, Sell Cheap' works in some markets and not in others…)

Select Analysis/Regression & Correlation/Simple Linear & Correlation

Choose 'Sales' as Outcome (Y axis) and Price as Predictor (X axis)

Shop	Sales	Price	Instore Advertising	Street Promotion	Local Radio
1	8600	24.99	2180	6400	12000
2	9100	18.99	2200	7800	11500
3	9400	24.99	2220	6800	12400
4	9500	24.99	2160	7000	13500
5	9800	18.99	2220	6500	13200
6	10700	18.99	2170	5000	13500
7	11200	18.99	2280	6800	13200
8	11400	18.99	2500	7200	13500
9	11400	18.99	2200	6000	13500
10	11700	18.99	2250	7400	12900
11	3800	30.99	2190	5000	11000
12	4900	30.99	2250	7500	12000
13	6100	24.99	1180	5400	11900
14	6500	30.99	2250	6000	12500
15	6900	30.99	2170	8200	12100
16	7300	30.99	2180	6500	14000
17	7400	20.99	2255	6100	12200
18	7600	30.99	2250	6800	12300
19	7800	18.99	2200	6000	13300
20	8100	20.99	2240	6900	10000
21	11800	30.99			

The Correlation Coefficient (Pearson's Product Moment r) = -0.61 ; the negative is fine, representing an inverse relationship: lower prices, higher sales. $p < .01$ The effect size - r2 - is .37; we shall look at the implications of this shortly.

Now take the 'plot regression' option. Apart from anything else, we want to make sure that the relationship is linear. It is linear. Another problem emerges, however: an outlier. One coordinate is well away from the other data and is theoretically dubious, selling at the highest price and yet is also selling well; let's not go there.

During data exploration, removing data just because it is inconvenient to you is unforgivable. We are now, however, in the business of making predictions, so it is reasonable to remove the outlier to improve the prediction model. We are interested in the generality of usual behaviour. In future calculations using this data set, do not use this outlier (conveniently placed at the bottom).

Now run the Regression again without the outlier (i.e., 20 items). The correlation is now –0.77, with an effect size of 0.59. With much more of the variance accounted for, we have a more valid tool for prediction.

Now we get to the point of this exercise: *interpolate X to Y*. In other words, put in a single value for Price and see its likely effect on Sales. For example, if we put up the price to 35, sales are likely to be a little over 4,500; if we drop the price to 15, sales are likely to rise to above 11,000; price = 25, sales = 7,800. Let's pass the calculator to the CEO…

Multiple Regression – multiple predictor variables against one criterion variable

Returning to our table, we may ask if price by itself is the only significant factor in determining the number of sales. Multiple regression allows one to build a *model* for effective prediction. We are interested in two main issues: does the addition of extra variables make an appreciable difference to predictions? And, if so, are some variables more useful than others?

Select Analysis/Regression & Correlation/Multiple Linear and ignore the invitations to use weights (too heavy at this stage of our development). Select *Sales* as the *Outcome (Y axis)* – remember just to choose the first 20, without the outlier – then select *Price, Instore Advertising, Street Promotion and Local Radio* as *Predictors*. The immediate screen is quite informative: Price, in an inverse way (r = -0.82), is seen to be significant (i.e., not a chance effect), but so is Local Radio.

To find out the answer to our first question, whether or not this makes an appreciable difference to our predictive model, select *Analysis of Variance* (and press 'calculate').

There is a significant effect, with the Multiple Correlation Coefficient R = 0.89 (our simple price/sales regression was –0.77). The effect size R^2 is .79 (referred to by StatsDirect as 79.5% of the variance), but it may be better to pay attention to the adjusted effect size of .74, or 74% of the variance. As the effect size of the simple regression was 59%, this model is a more effective one. In other words, we would do well to consider other factors in addition to price when predicting sales.

Before trying anything else, it may be worth checking for statistical safety. Calculate '*Residual plots*'. Residuals, essentially errors, are nicely spread around on both sides of the axis when correlated with Y and with our favoured variables (1 for prices and 4 for local radio) – this is fine, as they should be randomly spread. The almost straight line in the bottom graph is also fine, as a straight line on a Normal plot for residuals indicates that the errors are spread randomly. Also calculate '*Collinearity*': essentially, high collinearity means that variables are over-correlated against each other, possibly meaning that they may be measuring the same underlying construct; in such a case, we probably need to get rid of unnecessary variables. (Rather than fishing for results, one should only include variables that 'make sense'.) As it is, all variables show a high tolerance factor (good) and a low variance inflation factor (1 is good). Press '*Help*' if you want more guidance on these measurements.

Returning to the significance levels, it looks like a worthwhile move to refine our model by removing Instore Advertising and Street Promotion as less influential factors. So, now we go back and perform multiple regression with just price and local radio as predictors: *Analysis of Variance* gives a multiple correlation coefficient of 0.85, and an adjusted effect size of .69 (69%). Our two factors account for considerably more of the variance than the simple model. We do not seem to have lost much by removing the others, although one could always look for another relevant factor.

Having found a useful model, however, let us predict with it. Opt for *Prediction*. Use the left-hand text box to adjust values for the Predictor variables. If we alter the Price to 11.99 and put up our expenditure on local radio to 20,000 – using the left-hand box as a drop-down menu - then, after pressing 'calculate', the screen shows our sales soaring to over 18,000. The intervals cited underneath show the possibility of this varying somewhat…

MULTIPLE CORRELATION

One can also study the pattern of relationships between more than two variables. Bear in mind, however, that the more correlations you run that appear to be significant, the greater the chance that some of them are, in fact, the product of chance results. If each test has, say, a one in a hundred chance of being a fluke, then this rises as more tests are conducted. One highly conservative method to counter this is the Bonferroni technique: you multiply a correlation's p value by the number of comparisons to get an adjusted p value. If we take our sales example using all the variables there, the use of multiple regression will show us that the radio promotion p value is $p = 0.0076$; our comparisons numbering 10, we get 0.076. This is rather harsh and – this is the real world entering our calculations – almost certainly wrong; the Bonferroni is particularly fierce when applied to a large number of tests. If, however, we just look at sales, price and radio promotion, as recommended in our multiple regression example, we get a less impressive p value of 0.01, but we are only using 3 comparisons, giving an adjusted p value of 0.03.

Leaving aside the Bonferroni method, let us examine a *correlation matrix* involving our sales example: select Analysis/ Regression & Correlation/Principal Components/Correlation and use all 5 variables. If offered the opportunity to 'reverse scale option', say 'No' at the moment: negative correlations are meaningful in this example (high sales, low price); on other occasions, you may opt for reverse scaling where obverse relationships are irrelevant. Now ignore the initial screen (components, Eigenvalues, etc.): this will be discussed when we look at factor analysis. Opt for *Correlation Matrix* and 'Calculate'. (You may wish to copy the matrix to a workbook for clarity.)

Two common features of correlation matrices may be seen. Firstly, where a variable is matched against itself, a perfect correlation (1) is observed. Secondly, the two halves of the correlation matrix either side of the line of 1's are mirror images of each other, so you only need to pay attention to one of these triangles of data (the lower half is probably easier to look at).

In our example, we can see a large negative correlation between Sales and Price and a fairly large positive correlation between Sales and Radio promotion (supporting our previous decision to concentrate on these factors in multiple regression prediction). With regard to the effect size – how far the correlations account for the variance of the effect – you can work this out by squaring the correlation coefficient. -.767 * -.767 = .588: Price x Sales accounts for half the variance. 0.534 * .534 = .285: Price x Radio promotion is also influential. The other effect sizes would be much less impressive even if they were significant; it should be noted that the apparent paradox of statistically significant variables with negligible effect sizes is a commonplace and you will, at some point, have to make some difficult decisions about what is 'significant' when it comes to application in the real world.

Situations can be less clear than in our example. Several correlations, with a range of decent sized coefficients, may render 'eyeballing' of the correlation matrix a hopeless enterprise. Some subjective decisions can be made with the assistance of Exploratory Factor Analysis.

FACTOR ANALYSIS – A DATA REDUCTION METHODOLOGY

Exploratory Factor Analysis

Factor analysis is both a generic name for the extraction of underlying variables from data and for a specific technique. Here, we consider factor analysis in general. It should be noted that the reader may find this section more difficult than the earlier ones; believe it or not, you will find far more complex explanations of factor analysis elsewhere …

The basic point of exploratory factor analysis is to take several correlations and reduce a bulky conglomeration of variables into hopefully meaningful components, or *factors*. Factor analytic techniques try to find a structure in the relationships between variables, reducing the number of variables into a smaller number of components. If, for example, survey respondents declare a liking for several variables, you may want to find if there are a few common attitudes which account for many of the responses.

As usual, there are real world considerations. Avoid the poor practice of lumping together all the variables from a large study; put in those variables which you think are likely to be relevant. Also, note that the results should be inter-correlated to some extent: if there is no relationship, then there will be no common factors. On the other hand, too high a correlation between two variables may indicate that they measure the same thing; one should be removed before a factor analysis is conducted. There is serious debate about whether or not factors are merely statistical artefacts rather than meaningful entities. In practical terms, this can be resolved to some extent; as is usual when using statistical techniques, a lot depends upon having a sensible rationale for action rather than just pressing the button to see what happens.

There is a lot of literature on the process of factor analysis. The following, very brief explanation is not necessary for conducting the tests but may be helpful when you are confronted by reports on factor analysis. Firstly, a correlation matrix is formed from the data (as we looked at in the previous section). Secondly, factors are extracted, for example, using the Principal Components Analysis (PCA) technique. Thirdly, if you were using the *technique* called Factor Analysis, the factors would be *rotated*; as we do not use factor analysis here, rotation need not concern us, but a brief discussion can be found in the technical appendix later in this section.

Principal Components Analysis – A Factor Analytical Technique

PCA is a precursor to factor analysis the technique, but is now the most widely used method of factor analysis. The data below consists of 15 rows, representing observations (individuals, shops or other objects) and the 12 variables, A to L. The latter could be measures of business data, individuals' performance on different tests, etc. We want to see if there are any common underlying variables, how many there are, and how far each contributes to the variance.

A	B	C	D	E	F	G	H	I	J	K	L
82	92	61	28	25	16	79	54	60	43	28	61
41	44	67	51	81	45	62	61	32	57	54	67
41	72	71	74	79	30	85	57	40	51	41	39
93	84	58	43	42	15	70	70	76	69	14	20
86	92	48	54	36	26	72	69	67	59	14	26
39	53	51	75	48	42	94	84	69	58	19	39
54	45	89	54	56	42	89	60	49	47	35	40
88	98	58	27	35	11	70	62	72	57	15	33
78	97	69	53	41	12	72	67	54	46	26	42
66	92	63	76	60	28	56	43	21	39	80	83
72	95	55	79	39	35	60	53	32	53	60	74
71	87	65	73	70	13	80	65	64	65	20	33
76	80	52	67	60	16	67	52	53	54	51	56
47	61	76	45	79	36	56	63	56	55	38	51
84	81	56	73	61	48	47	39	14	34	75	87

Three points about the raw data. There must be at least 100 observations. There should also be 5 times as many subjects (rows) as variables; these rules are ignored here for brevity's sake. Also, it is helpful to place together variables that you think are related.

Using the data above, select Analysis/Regression & Correlation/Principal Components/Correlation. You will then be asked about 'scale reversal'. Saying 'yes' removes negative signs from correlations, which may be helpful when negatives are merely an artefact of survey coding, for example mixtures of 1-5 and 5-1 scales, and, therefore, irrelevant. In this case, however, say 'no' and leave the negatives in.

The main screen appears as follows:

Principal components (correlation)

Component	Eigenvalue (SVD)	Proportion	Cumulative
1	5.279569	44%	44%
2	3.22758	26.9%	70.89%
3	1.200434	10%	80.9%
4	0.836621	6.97%	87.87%
5	0.724655	6.04%	93.91%
6	0.259211	2.16%	96.07%
7	0.183885	1.53%	97.6%
8	0.137727	1.15%	98.75%
9	0.075948	0.63%	99.38%
10	0.040318	0.34%	99.72%
11	0.032293	0.27%	99.99%
12	0.001759	0.01%	100%

Components 1 to 12 on the left are generated by the software and are not of importance, except in showing the order of size of potential components, from largest to smallest. Any components could conceivably be considered to be factors and we need a way of deciding on a cut-off. As will be discussed, this can be a matter of judgement, dependent on known attributes, but the reading of Eigenvalues is a useful statistically based cut-off procedure: generally speaking, we only take account of components with Eigenvalues of 1 or more, so in this case, there would appear to be three discernible factors.

'Proportion' shows each component's contribution to the variance; as will be noted by the 'Cumulative' column, the three largest factors account for almost 81% of the variance.

In addition to the main screen, opt for 'Correlation Matrix' (and 'Calculate').

Where there are several variables in a correlation matrix, the StatsDirect matrix may be cramped: if you copy this to the workbook, the matrix can be seen clearly.

	A	B	C	D	E	F	G	H	I	J	K	L
A	1											
B	**0.797284**	1										
C	**-0.46107**	**-0.48565**	1									
D	**-0.33809**	-0.08856	-0.15265	1								
E	**-0.67964**	**-0.58678**	**0.446427**	**0.40282**	1							
F	**-0.60871**	**-0.7016**	0.199722	**0.399446**	**0.439997**	1						
G	**-0.30214**	-0.27815	0.187951	-0.05097	-0.17408	-0.16479	1					
H	-0.22107	-0.26694	-0.0653	-0.20526	-0.16758	-0.14595	**0.64422**	1				
I	0.229777	0.097546	-0.14843	**-0.53182**	**-0.42052**	**-0.58423**	**0.575239**	**0.788691**	1			
J	-0.00488	-0.09652	-0.18292	-0.16515	0.022569	**-0.32551**	**0.332817**	**0.721459**	**0.721477**	1		
K	-0.17893	-0.0624	0.05081	**0.523998**	**0.401355**	**0.507242**	**-0.65347**	**-0.8277**	**-0.95151**	**-0.67777**	1	
L	-0.10216	0.011382	-0.05177	**0.356243**	0.197358	**0.472773**	**-0.65027**	**-0.78599**	**-0.87921**	**-0.74118**	**0.924237**	1

The upper half of the computer-generated matrix has been removed from the chart above, as a whole matrix mirrors about the leading diagonal and can play tricks with the eyes, providing a mirage of imaginary clusters. The cells have also been conditionally formatted; any figure above .3 or below -.3 is in a darker font. Positive correlations of less than .3 and negative correlations larger than -.3 tend not to be meaningful in this context.

Previously, I recommended the practice of placing variables which are particularly likely to be related to each other into adjacent columns of the raw data. This allows easy viewing of any correlation clusters. Guessing which variables are closely related before subjecting the data is always a good idea. As has been discussed, you should have some rationale behind your data selections, but, in the case of the correlation matrix, failure to align the variables will require an even more intense eyeballing of the data. When looking at your own data, however, the nature of the factors should become clearer.

In this case, we can see that variables K and L are highly correlated, with strong negative relationships with several other variables; often a construct may be partially defined by opposites. A and B are also highly correlated, with a grouping of positive relationships. The guidance from the Eigenvalues, seeing that we have two very influential factors, seems to be borne out.

Other clusters occur as well. The Eigenvalues suggest that a third factor is likely to have explanatory power. When dealing with variables in real life, however, we are likely to have more of a clue as to which factor and how important this is. Again, such real world considerations are likely to inform us whether or not the smaller fourth or fifth factors have any meaning or are merely the mathematical constructs implied in the list of components with Eigenvalues below 1.

As you might suspect, in spite of all the calculations, exploratory factor analysis has a considerable element of subjectivity, an art as well as a science if you like.

CONFIRMATORY FACTOR ANALYSIS

As a relatively advanced technique, CFA is not going to be covered in any detail here.

Essentially, Exploratory Factor Analysis, as above, looks at data in a 'bottom-up' way and attempts to create a model of underlying factors.

Confirmatory Factor Analysis works 'top-down'. It uses data to confirm or test factorial models. One can test models against each other, for example. One can test the reliability of a model; in the example given, you might try out new sets of data to see if the three- or four-factor model is the more useful, or if the entire model is misleading.

Factor Analysis – A Short Technical Appendix *Factors* – also known as latent variables, dimensions, or core constructs.
Eigenvalue – represents the total amount of variance contributed to by a factor. Deciding to use Eigenvalues of 1 and above is known as *the Kaiser Criterion.* Eigenvalues, however, are a *guide*, particularly for when the divide between potential factors is less than clear. Depending upon the meaningfulness of the potential categories, one could have argued for four factors in our example. In real world decision-making, the number of factors should be influenced by theory and/or empirical evidence. All other things being equal, however, a theory with fewer factors should be preferred in borderline cases.

Rotation – used in the technique called 'Factor Analysis'. Whereas the positions of clusters on X and Y axes make a lot of sense in univariate (one-variable) statistics, the immediate position of variables in multivariate statistics is not particularly meaningful. The point is that the initial position of a set of factors on graphical 'X Y' axes may not lead to sensible clusters: a three dimensional concept, as it were, is placed on a two-dimensional chart, rendering the direction of the axes largely irrelevant. The constellations of stars could be a useful metaphor: these appear to be real formations but are, in fact, individual stars at diverse distances merely clustered according to the viewer's perspective. Rotation is a legitimate way of adjusting the position of the clusters to achieve what textbooks refer to as '*simple structure*', a tight and meaningful separation of factors. (Simple structure is an elusive concept; before running a factor analysis, you are also presented with the rather complex question of which type of rotation to choose, orthogonal or oblique, etc!)

TALKING POINT

We have already established that apparently strong correlations can be coincidental. Do too many tests and that five-in-a-hundred fluke is increasingly likely to occur.

Another perceived weakness of correlations is that they do not prove cause and effect. This is, of course, a problem. As an example, let us say that we have established a reliable relationship between confidence in the government and high levels of spending. Are we sure that perceived stability leads to higher spending? Or, could it be that high disposable incomes lead to political complacency? Or, is there a *mediating factor* which needs to be taken into account, such as unemployment?

One way of sorting out the problem is to run experiments or quasi-experiments. It is not always practical to do so, however. *Triangulation* of methods can be also be used; different aspects of a problem may be subjected to different forms of analysis to see if the original theory may be disproven. Confirmatory Factor Analysis, for example, could be used to test the given relationship, looking at different variables to examine the direction of an effect or to provide more explanatory models. Methods such as Structural Equation Modelling are also used to examine the direction of correlational effects.

This table of tests of relationships is not exhaustive, but refers to tests used in this chapter.

N.b. *Non-parametric tests can be used with 'parametric' data.*

Purpose	Number of Conditions	Data	Test
Correlation	2 2 More than 2	Non-parametric Parametric Parametric	Spearman Pearson Multiple Correlation
Prediction	2 2 More than 2	Non-parametric Parametric Parametric	Non-parametric linear regression Simple linear regression Multiple Regression
Significance levels	More than 2	Non-parametric	Bonferroni Test
Data reduction (exploratory factor analysis)	Multi-variable (must have several conditions)	Parametric	Principal Components Analysis (PCA)

CHAPTER NINE

THE TIME UNTIL EVENTS: SURVIVAL ANALYSIS

Here, we are interested in the area of statistics known as *Survival Analysis*.

Survival Analysis is concerned with how long it takes for an outcome, or *event*, to take place among a range of individuals. It focuses on the interval between the starting point - for example, the completion of a course of treatment – and the event; this interval is known as the *survival time, observation period* or *follow-up period.*

Traditionally, the events of interest have been the deaths of patients after a therapeutic intervention, hence the term 'survival analysis', but this range of techniques can be used much more widely. We can look at many other outcomes, positive and negative, such as employees resigning after the completion of a reorganisation initiative, staff promotions after a training course or the consequences of changes in taxation laws on such events as students graduating, university drop-outs and couples being married.

We are interested in learning about the survival time. Do events tend to accelerate after a particular period of time? Are there phases during which events tend to cluster? What proportion of individuals are affected in a particular phase?

It is also possible that we may wish to contrast different samples. Does the group on a special training programme truly have a different promotion rate from a control group on a traditional course? Will drop-out rates for an employment rehabilitation scheme differ according to different levels of support?

Other ways of measuring event rates could be considered, for example the graphical representation of averages or using the predictive power of linear regression. Survival analysis, however, has a range of advantages. It provides a far more informative analysis of the process under investigation. Non-linear patterns are not a problem; note, for example, that if one is looking at mortality, then there will inevitably be sizeable shifts from the average at both the beginning and the end of the follow-up period. Crucially, however, survival analysis accounts for missing information, known as *censored events*.

Censored information is that which the researcher can only guess at. This includes cases where the event fails to occur until after the follow-up period has expired; the fact, for example, that a cancer sufferer does not die within the survival time does not mean that he may not die from cancer after observations have been concluded. Similarly, individuals who have withdrawn from the study or with whom researchers have lost contact (*loss to follow-up*), may or may not experience the pertinent event. Even when we are certain that events will have taken place (we are all dead in the long run, said Keynes), we can not assume that we know when.

If we omit censored data, or count it as having the same duration as the latest recorded event, then we underestimate the effect under investigation. Although we could negate the time distortions by just focusing on events, we would lose the considerable richness of data provided by looking at duration.

Survival analysis measures the occurrence of events in terms of the duration of time in which they take place. It also takes into account censored data. This is the case when data is missing both during and after the monitoring period; both of these are called 'right censored data'. One should avoid introducing 'left censored data', where complications precede the survival time; some procedures can be put in place to deal with this, but we can't be dealing with it here.

Some assumptions about the data are required by survival analysis. Continuous data is required; this is usually days in the case of the Kaplan-Meier Survival Function. Longer gaps such as years should be measured by the Follow-Up Life Table. Each record must be a different individual; that is, you don't include the same person more than once. Censoring should be random; you must not exclude individuals from the survival period because they seem to be a particularly high (or low) risk. The event should be categorical; either they're dead or they're alive, cured or not, promoted or not, lapsed or not.

THE KAPLAN-MEIER SURVIVAL FUNCTION

The beauty of the Kaplan-Meier is the intuitiveness of the survival plot. Its steepness shows whether or not the probability of an event – e.g. promotion – is high or low, whether or not this accelerates or decelerates over time and differences between groups of patients under different conditions.

Firstly, however, we must prepare the data. This is ordered chronologically. One column of data holds the time number, often the number of days in which the person was observed. This is either the day in which the event occurred or the last observation day before the person became censored; individuals who go to the end of the period without the event occurring are given the number of the last day of the observation.

In each case, another column deems the event to have occurred (1) or to have been censored (0). If more than one treatment condition is to be examined, then another column is prepared, with a number for the group (1, 2, 3, etc). If there is more than one group, ordering of the data should be chronological.

Let us start with a very simple example. A management course has been completed among a group of staff at a similar level. We are interested in subsequent promotions. The cohort is deliberately small here, as we are interested in introducing this form of analysis rather than concerning ourselves with statistical significance or organisational meaningfulness.

Days	Promotions	We have a cohort of 12.
40	1	The first promotion takes place on the fortieth day.
60	1	
62	1	
80	1	
85	1	
108	1	Subsequent promotions take place until day 108.
108	1	
115	0	Censored data; perhaps the person has left the organization.
140	1	Another promotion on day 140.
160	0	Censored data again on day 160.
180	0	The remaining 2 of our cohort are not promoted on the last
180	0	day of observation, day 180.

After copying the first two columns onto a StatsDirect workbook, select Analysis/Survival Analysis/Kaplan-Meier. When prompted to ‘select data for Times’, select the Days column and press OK. When prompted to 'select data for Death/Events or Censored {0}', select the Promotions column and press OK. As we have not separated our cohort into groups, press 'Cancel' when asked for 'Group Identifier'.

Opt for 'No' to 'save estimates and CIs'. (Although it is often useful to declare Confidence Intervals, i.e. that you are 95% confident that results are within certain bounds, it may not be particularly useful here.) After sending the details to a report sheet, select 'show event markers' as a survival plot option; although you may not want this in the future, it helps here in our introduction.

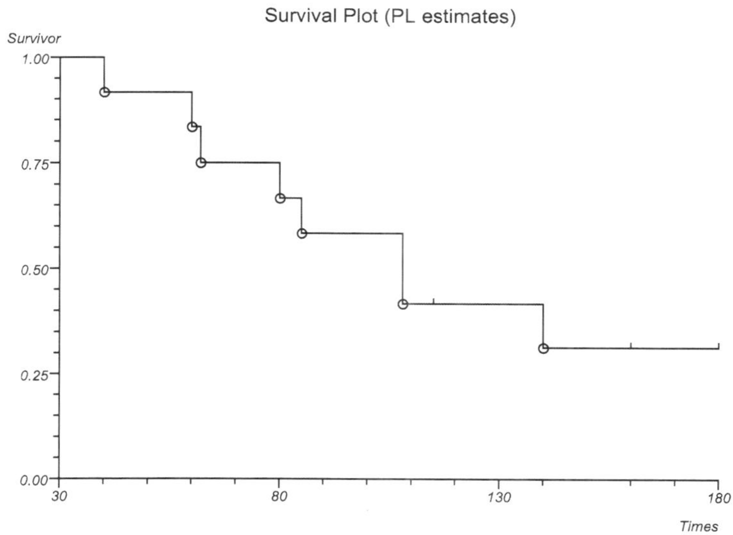

The event markers are the nodules at the bottom of each 'stair rung'; there are only 7 to be seen, as two events occur on the same day (108); as can be seen, a steeper drop occurs about midway along the time line. The censored events appear as upright marks along the horizontal lines; Kaplan-Meier takes these into account in making calculations but makes no assumptions about the effect, the rate of promotions.

The calculations of the likelihood of an event happening can be seen to have been worked out on the plot. It will be noted that the upright, or y axis, runs from 0 to 1, from zero to 100% of the individuals in the study. At 1, we have 100% of our cohort unaffected. After the first event, after 40 days, it looks like a bit over 90% of the cohort are unaffected, when we look at the figures ('S' in the table shown), we find that this is 91.667%. If we call it 92%, then we can say that the probability of promotion after 40 days is approximately 8% (100%-92%). Note that in real life, we would not make such extrapolations so early in such a small sample.

Then we look at the middle of the upright (y) axis and look across to the intersect. This is the median survival time, 108 days. This is only a 'point estimate' of duration, however; it may not be all that helpful to give this. The confidence interval median survival time may be more helpful, giving the most central figures. One way is to read off the days on the x axis relating to 75% and 25% on the y axis, or cite one of the statistics given in the read-out, the Brookmeyer-Crowley, a robust non-parametric statistic but which should not be used where events tend to happen on the same day, and the Andersen statistic.

Kaplan-Meier survival estimates (columns beyond 'S' have been omitted)

Time	At risk	Dead	Censored	S [Survival]	
40	12	1	0	0.916667	[92%]
60	11	1	0	0.833333	[84%]
62	10	1	0	0.75	[75%]
80	9	1	0	0.666667	[67%]
85	8	1	0	0.583333	[58%]
108	7	2	0	0.416667	[42%]
115	5	0	1	0.416667	

140	4	1	0	0.3125	[31%]
160	3	0	1	0.3125	
180	2	0	2	0.3125	

Median survival time = 108
Andersen 95% CI for median survival time = 69.506329 to 146.493671
Brookmeyer-Crowley 95% CI for median survival time = 80 to 180

It is perfectly acceptable, however, to use the 'S' figures, looking at the graph to maintain common sense, when we want to describe the effect. Here (with a bigger sample), we could say that after 62 days, there would appear to be a 25% likelihood of promotion (100% - 75%), and a 68% (100% - 42%) likelihood after 108 days. Note that the likelihood doesn't change after day 115, a censored event.

Now we move to a more complicated sample. After completion of a new rehabilitation programme for young offenders, we have 2 samples: members of the experimental group undertook the programme, with the control group undergoing standard procedures within the youth justice system. The follow-up period is 90 days. In each case, we have measured days until the event, committing a fresh criminal offence, or the last record.

Experimental group (15 participants):
27, 29 (C), 40, 54, 60, 72, 83, 84, 88, 90 (C), 90 (C), 90 (C), 90 (C), 90 (C), 90 (C).

Control group (15 participants):
16, 17, 18, 20, 22, 25, 25, 30 (C), 53, 71, 84, 86, 90 (C), 90 (C), 90 (C).

Expt = 1; Ctrl = 2	Days	Reoffend	We enter the data together, for comparison
2	16	1	on the plot, to examine the data as a whole.
2	17	1	
2	18	1	
2	20	1	Offences start to occur in the control group
2	22	1	after the first two weeks post-rehabilitation.
2	25	1	
2	25	1	
1	27	1	One offence in the experimental group.
1	29	0	Two individuals have either withdrawn from
2	30	0	the programme or otherwise lost to follow-up.
1	48	1	
2	53	1	
1	54	1	Some more offences occur as the weeks go by,
1	60	1	in both groups.
2	71	1	
1	72	1	
1	83	1	
1	84	1	
2	84	1	

2	86	1	
1	88	1	
1	90	0	Six members of the experimental group survive
1	90	0	the observation period without offending (n.b.
1	90	0	Kaplan-Meier, during the calculations, does not
1	90	0	ignore the possibility of a future offence).
1	90	0	
1	90	0	
2	90	0	Three members of the control group also
2	90	0	survive the follow-up period without offending.
2	90	0	

Select Analysis/Survival Analysis/Kaplan-Meier. When prompted to 'select data for Times', select the Days column. When prompted to 'select data for Death/Events or Censored {0}', select the Relapse column. For the moment, press 'Cancel' when asked for 'Group Identifier', as it seems reasonable to look at the data overall. As before, opt for 'No' to 'save estimates and CIs'; this time, we'll ignore 'show event markers' as a survival plot option.

Kaplan-Meier survival estimates

Time	At risk	Dead	Censored	S
16	30	1	0	0.966667

17	29	1	0	0.933333
18	28	1	0	0.9
20	27	1	0	0.866667
22	26	1	0	0.833333
25	25	2	0	0.766667
27	23	1	0	0.733333
29	22	0	1	0.733333
30	21	0	1	0.733333
48	20	1	0	0.696667
53	19	1	0	0.66
54	18	1	0	0.623333
60	17	1	0	0.586667
71	16	1	0	0.55
72	15	1	0	0.513333
83	14	1	0	0.476667
84	13	2	0	0.403333
86	11	1	0	0.366667
88	10	1	0	0.33
90	9	0	9	0.33

One thing to note is the number of censored events at the end of the row of figures. In general, a high number of these can mean that a lot of individuals do indeed fail to experience the event in question; but an alternative explanation can be that the follow-up period is just not long enough to make sufficient observations. We can say, however, that there is a 51% survival likelihood after 72 days (49% are likely to relapse by then).

On the other hand, 33% are likely to continue without offending up to or beyond 90 days. This is also clear in the survival plot, which also indicates something else. A steep re-offending trend appears in the third week after follow-up, with a fairly pronounced trend towards the end of the follow-up period.

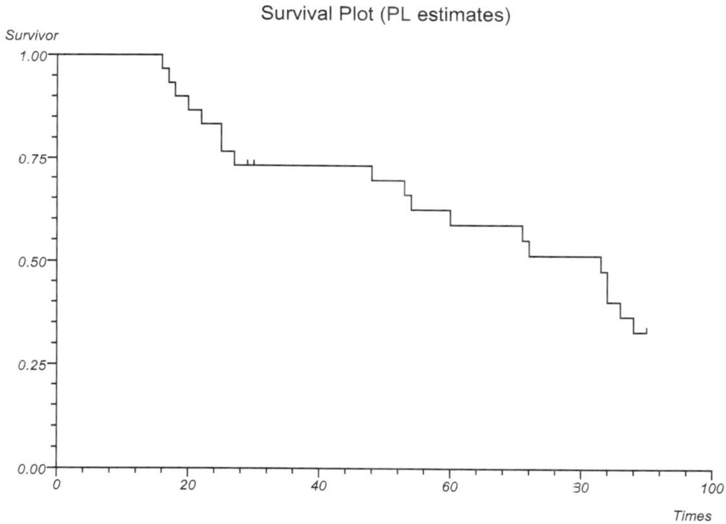

The hazard rate plot, which shows the relative acceleration of risk, demonstrates this.

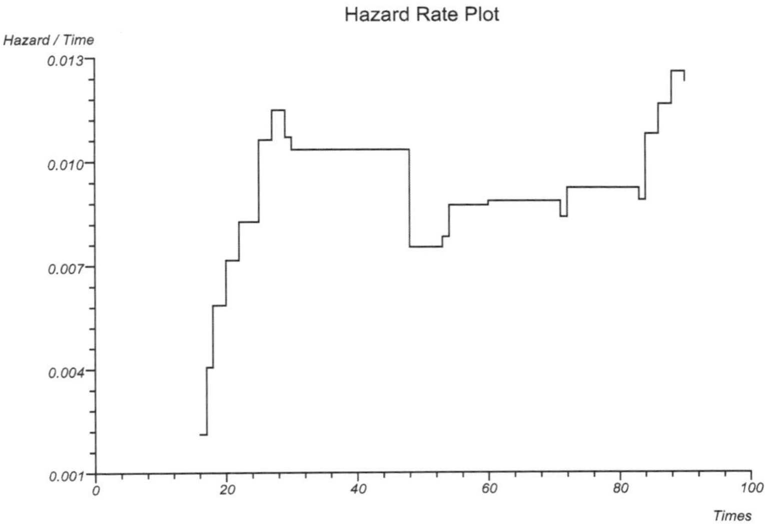

Let us now compare the two groups. This time, when using Kaplan-Meier and asked to 'select data for Group Identifier', select the group column (here, 'Expt = 1; Ctrl = 2').

Kaplan-Meier survival estimates

Expt1Crtl2 = 2

Time	At risk	Dead	Censored	S
16	15	1	0	0.933333
17	14	1	0	0.866667
18	13	1	0	0.8
20	12	1	0	0.733333
22	11	1	0	0.666667
25	10	2	0	0.533333
30	8	0	1	0.533333
53	7	1	0	0.457143

71	6	1	0	0.380952
84	5	1	0	0.304762
86	4	1	0	0.228571
90	3	0	3	0.228571

Median survival time = 53
Andersen 95% CI for median survival time = 8.959823 to 97.040177
Brookmeyer-Crowley 95% CI for median survival time = 22 to 84

Mean survival time (95% CI) [limit: 90 on 86] = 52.504762 (35.664489 to 69.345034)

Expt1Crtl2 = 1

Time	At risk	Dead	Censored	S
27	15	1	0	0.933333
29	14	0	1	0.933333
48	13	1	0	0.861538
54	12	1	0	0.789744
60	11	1	0	0.717949
72	10	1	0	0.646154
83	9	1	0	0.574359
84	8	1	0	0.502564
88	7	1	0	0.430769
90	6	0	6	0.430769

Median survival time = 88
Andersen 95% CI for median survival time = 78.962093 to 97.037907

Brookmeyer-Crowley 95% CI for median survival time = 60 to 90

Mean survival time (95% CI) [limit: 90 on 88] = 75.676923 (65.005153 to 86.348693)

We note at the bottom of each table the number of people who have lasted up to or beyond the 90 day observation period: three in the control group (Expt1Crtl2 = 2) and six in the experimental group (Expt1Crtl2 = 1). There are also clear differences between the groups in the rest of the survival data. Little more than 50% of the control group are likely to survive (S) without offending after 30 days (S = 53%; there is 47% chance of an event, an offence, at this time). In the meantime, there is very little movement among the experimental group. By the end of follow-up, only 23% of the controls are likely to survive without incident (77% reoffending likelihood), compared to 46% of the experimental group. The other statistics show a similar story (note that the median survival time is generally deemed to be of more use in survival analysis than the mean).

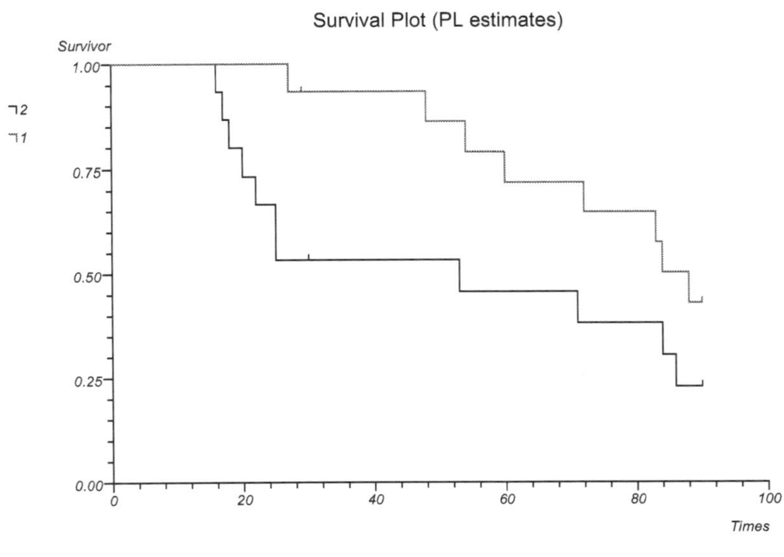

The survival plot shows an interesting story. Group 2, the control group, reoffend very quickly, within about a week. If this is usual criminologically, then fine, it shows that the new rehabilitation scheme would appear to help participants to avoid this slough; it would be worth checking, however, in case something unusual affected this particular group of young people at this time. There would appear to be a clear difference between the groups over time, although there is a similar decline towards the end, which does rather suggest that the observation time should have been somewhat longer.

The hazard plot shows a clear increase in risk among the control group in the early period. Increased risk appears at the end for both groups. At the very least, we should be concerned about possible vulnerability of all young ex-offenders during this period of time.

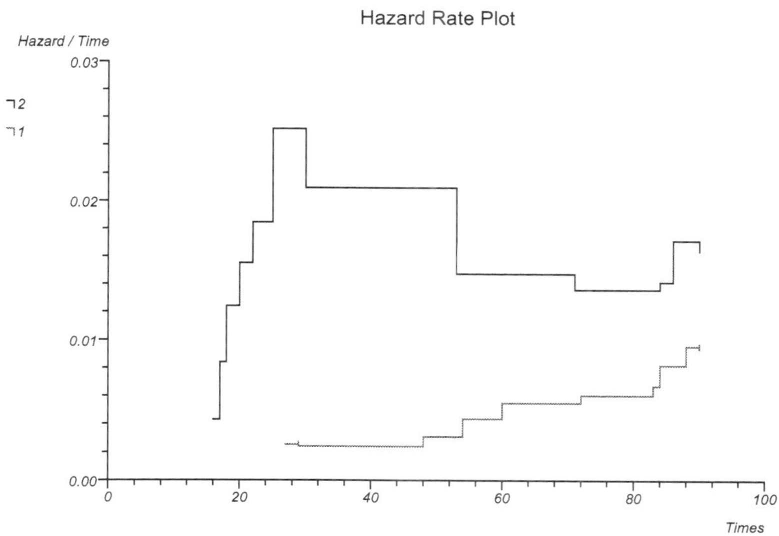

TESTS OF SIGNIFICANCE IN SURVIVAL ANALYSIS

Before seeing whether or not the differences in our example are significant, we need to consider the tests of significance offered by StatsDirect.

Peto's log-rank test is best when testing a survival curve throughout its entire course and is more sensitive when the two groups show consistently similar patterns (the first set of data on the Survival sheet of StatsDirect's test file responds in such a way).

The Peto-Prentice Wilcoxon test is considered to be a very reliable test for use in Survival Analysis.

The Gehan-Breslow Wilcoxon test is considered to be more sensitive to differences between groups at early stages. This test can, however, tend towards Type Two errors (judging results not to be significant when they are – a 'False Negative'; the opposite is a Type One error, a 'False Positive', seeing significance when it should be absent).

The Tarone-Ware Wilcoxon test is preferred where survival curves intersect or move away from each other.

Select Analysis/Survival Analysis/Log-Rank & Wilcoxon. The order of data selection is a little different here. First, 'select data for Group Identifier'; here this is Expt1Ctrl2. Then, 'select data for times'; here, Days. Then, 'select data for Deaths/Events or Censored {0}'; here, Relapse. Opt for 'Cancel' when asked for to 'select data for Strata'.

You would use stratification if you had different conditions to contrast (e.g. young with drug problems and without drug problems would be considered stratified data). If dealing with stratified data, you would enter data like so, with stratified data on the right (the variable is Drg1Nodrg2: 1 = drug history, 2 = no drug history).

Expt = 1; Ctrl = 2	Days	Relapse	Drg1Nodrg2
2	16	1	1
2	17	1	2
1	18	0	2
2	20	1	1
etc	etc	etc	etc

Returning to this study, however, the most pertinent tests of significance are the Peto-Prentice and Gehan-Breslow. Both show significant between-group differences, at $p < .05$

(If we look for interest's sake at the less appropriate tests, the differences appear, unsurprisingly, to be insignificant under the Log-Rank (Peto) test; $p < .1$ This reflects the differences between the patterns of the two groups. Tarone-Ware, however, shows $p < .05$, suggesting the potential dangers of dredging.)

THE FOLLOW-UP LIFE TABLE

Generally speaking, if you can use the Kaplan-Meier, with its richness of data, you should. However, in spite of being a non-parametric method, Kaplan-Meier is designed to look at continuous data. If we are looking at intervals, such as months, quarters and years, then a Follow-Up Life Table should be considered. The minimum sample size for a life table, in terms of the number of participants starting the study, is 30, although some authorities recommend at least 100; life tables are typically used with thousands.

As an example, let us say that we are interested in how long convicted drink-drivers remain unconvicted after regaining their licences. The initial sample is 200 in number. For the sake of brevity, we use a rather short observation period.

Years	Reconvicted	Withdrawn	The first column carries the intervals (these
0	60	18	do not have to be 1,2,3, etc).
1	35	3	The second column shows actual events.
2	20	5	The third has 'Lost to follow-up'/censored.
3	15	2	N.B. the table does not contain the whole sample;
4	5	1	36 were not convicted in the follow-up period.

Select Analysis/Survival Analysis/Follow-Up Life Table

At the prompts, select the Years column for 'Times', the Reconvicted column for 'Deaths' and Withdrawn for 'Withdrawals'. You are then asked the number who started the study; StatsDirect offers by default the total given within the table, but we enter 200 as the actual sample, as we have survivors who are not included in the columns.

FOLLOW-UP LIFE TABLE

Interval	Deaths	Withdrawn	At risk	Adj. at risk	P(death)
0 to 1	60	18	200	191	0.314136
1 to 2	35	3	122	120.5	0.290456
2 to 3	20	5	84	81.5	0.245399
3 to 4	15	2	59	58	0.258621
4 up	5	1	42	*	*

Interval	P(survival)	Survivors (lx%)	SD of lx%	95% CI for lx%
0 to 1	0.685864	100	*	* to *
1 to 2	0.709544	68.586387	12.986565	61.485147 to 74.651522
2 to 3	0.754601	48.66503	10.569952	41.230443 to 55.685715
3 to 4	0.741379	36.722691	9.874568	29.650539 to 43.801528
4 up	*	27.225444	9.661451	20.757746 to 34.076007

The first part of the table does not just reflect our input. As in the Kaplan-Meier, the risk is adjusted. Instead of working out reconvictions (Deaths) as a fraction of the entire sample (in the first interval, 60/200 = 0.3), the table adjusts the sample as if half of the withdrawn sample were reconvicted, giving a slightly higher 'death'/reconviction rate (60/191 = 0.314). When this sum is subtracted from 100, we get the survival rate for that particular interval (0.686).

To look at the cumulative effects, rather than survival rates for a particular period, we need to look at the Confidence Intervals on the right (95% CI, i.e. p < .05%) and describe them year by year. Therefore we can say with a degree of confidence that 1 year after the operation, between 61.5% and 74.7% of the drivers are likely to have continued to drive without reconvictions (the point estimate of the individual survival rate being 68.6%), falling to between 41.2% to 55.7% after 2 years, and so on.

TALKING POINT

The statistical methods referred to in this chapter are often referred to by the overall title of Survival Analysis. This reflects its most familiar usage in health statistics, the tracking of the survival rate of patients over time; this is made manifest in StatsDirect's use of 'deaths' when events are referred to in analysis readouts. Having said that, I feel that it is more useful to consider it as the study of the time until events, as we are not necessarily discussing life and death and can be measuring events which are positive and not necessarily dramatic. Other terms are indeed used, including 'time to event analysis' and, in sociology and economics, 'duration analysis'.

This table of survival analysis techniques only refers to tests used in this chapter.
N.b. *Non-parametric tests can be used with 'parametric' data.*

Test	Number of groups	Data	Purpose
Kaplan-Meier	1 or more	Non-parametric. Large and small sample. Data must be continuous (i.e. not less frequent than days).	Tracking events over time
Follow-up Life Table	1	Non-parametric. Large samples. Interval data (e.g. months, quarters, years).	Tracking events over time

Log-rank & Wilcoxon tests	2 or more	Non-parametric. For usage differences between Peto Log-Rank, and variations of Wilcoxon tests Peto-Prentice, Gehan-Breslow and Tarone-Ware, see earlier notes in this section.	Testing significance of group differences under Kaplan-Meier

You will find that StatsDirect offers other tests, extending survival analysis to multivariate data (Cox's Regression, Wei-Lachin). The program also provides tests relating to parametric distributions (Probit, Logit, etc). I feel, however, that these methods are not appropriate for an introductory text; indeed, they require the assistance of a statistician.

SECTION THREE:
BEYOND THE TESTS

CHAPTER TEN

EXERCISES

Question 1

40 tasters of two fruit drink products, OurDrink and RivalDrink, were asked which they would *prefer* to give their children. No 'abstaining' was allowed, from drinking or preference. 26 of the tasters answered in favour of OurDrink. What test should be used and what is the outcome? Accept a significance level of $p < .05$

Question 2

Wanting to find if women were more likely to take a different view of a policy than men, ratings of the policy were examined. What method was appropriate?

Question 3

Assuming a proven relationship between scores on an admission test and subsequent pass rates on a course, what method should we use to choose applicants?

Question 4

You are looking at the relationship between gender and management level in an industry. The numbers at each hierarchical level are as follows.

	ChiefExecs	SeniorTeam	Middle	FirstLine
Female	6	11	20	30
Male	8	18	16	32

What method should we use? Are there significant differences?

Question 5

Three different tax policies are currently being considered. Each politician has been asked for the policy they are most in favour of. There are three political parties. Of the Red Party, 100 favoured Policy A, 230 favoured Policy B, and 150 favoured Policy C. The Blue Party favoured Policies A, B and C as follows: 600, 400, 100. The Green Party favoured Policy A with 180 votes, with 120 for Policy B, and 100 for C.

What design should be adopted? Are the test results significant?

Question 6

The correlation matrix for a mass of data includes many correlations at .9. What should you do?

Question 7

Is a correlation coefficient of .2 significant?

ANSWERS TO EXERCISES

Answer 1

Use the Sign Test. The 26:14 ratio would be significant if a one-tailed level of significance was adopted. But do we really have preconceptions about whether or not people would be inclined to like one product more than the other? I would argue for the two-tailed level of significance. If we adopt this, then we are unable to consider the result to be significantly different from chance.

Answer 2

Mann-Whitney examines the differences between two sets of individuals on rating scales. (With great confidence in the rating scales, the unpaired t-test could be used.)

Answer 3

Regression. The individual's admission score would be used to predict his or her likely grade. Given the likelihood of plenty of data, simple regression would be preferred to non-parametric regression.

Answer 4

Chi-square. Not significant.

Answer 5

	Policy A	**Policy B**	**Policy C**
Red Party	100	230	150
Blue Party	600	400	100
Green Party	180	120	100

Chi-square. Clearly significant

Answer 6

Check for collinearity. It is likely that some variables are saying the same thing. Examine the content of the items and consider removing items which have over-similar meanings. You do want some similarities but not duplication. After such a cull with a lowering of collinearity, you may consider a type of factor analysis to reduce data further, then going into more in-depth examination of the correlations.

Answer 7

Especially when dealing with large amounts of data, this sort of correlation coefficient can indeed be accompanied by an acceptable p value. More to the point is how useful is an effect size of .04? In some cases, 4% of the variance is important, in others not.

CHAPTER ELEVEN

REPORTING IN APPLIED RESEARCH

Please note that the recommendations in this particular chapter are for people analysing data in applied settings, not for people who are preparing academic research papers. The latter are usually able to refer to their college's or professional body's specifications; failing that, most books on research methods should help.

In the discussion below, I shall refer to three levels of sophistication of the likely readers of your research. Such a reader may be the commissioner of research, or a line manager within your own organisation or an external body. The sophisticated reader will know as much as you do about the use of statistical methods, and probably more. The intermediate reader is likely to, at least, remember about significance levels from their own studies in the past. The unsophisticated reader will not necessarily understand the difference between statistical significance and the everyday use of the word; p levels will mean nothing.

WRITTEN REPORTING

Firstly, in reporting significant results, we dispense with the null hypothesis. Although I explained the term while explaining methodology, the lay reader is not concerned with such apparent paradoxes. You merely report that the result is 'significant' (or 'not significant'). If your audience is relatively sophisticated, you may put it as being 'significant ($p < .05$)' or 'significant to level $p < .05$'; with an intermediate level of sophistication, the first time such a citation is made, you may explain that this means that the likelihood of the results being a matter of chance are only 5 in a hundred. You would only consider using references to 'two-tailed' or 'one-tailed' hypotheses for the sophisticated readers; even for such an audience, a discussion of whether or not the effect was expected in a particular direction would be helpful.

Following on from this point is effect size. The term effect size would only be used with a sophisticated audience. It should be noted that until very recently, the concept (or proportion of variance) was rarely mentioned in introductory books. The intermediate reader could be told that this is a 'large', 'medium-sized' or 'small' effect; do not bother with $\mathbf{r}^2$ (or *d* or any other references to the names of actual statistics). Be even more sparing with unsophisticated audiences; mentions of particularly large (or small) effects are sufficient.

Thirdly, only cite the statistical tests used on a regular basis with sophisticated audiences. With the intermediate reader, the occasional mention of Friedman, or whatever, should only be given in parentheses – "the result was significant to $p <.05$ (Friedman)" just to impress a little. Don't cite at all with the lowest level of reader.

Fourthly, unlike in academic research, the reader does *not* want to know how you organised your data (unless this is strictly of relevance to the organisation). You should still of course, record your methods so that they can be replicated as necessary. In the case of removing outliers, however, the sophisticated reader may be informed; they are likely to understand the relevance or otherwise of such data.

In general terms, just provide the reader with relevant results, ones which have a bearing on the purpose of the research. It should not resemble an academic thesis, should not be long and, while not an entertainment, should be readable and cogent.

VERBAL REPORTING

If using slide-show presentations, try to keep the information interesting. At the least, have clauses sliding in from the side. Don't have large slabs of text if you can possibly avoid this.

A good idea is to have one idea, with a chart and possibly the relevant statistic (bearing in mind the audience), on one page.

TALKING POINT

Clear categorisation and knowing what to omit are central to good report-writing. Unfortunately, however, there are two ways of considering this point. Making things clearer to the audience is clearly one. Playing to the audience is another: there can be a tension between the audience's needs and objectivity. A current maxim in UK research circles (circa 2006) suggests that, in many cases, researchers are not helping to develop evidence-based policy so much as producing policy-based evidence! May your ideals go with you…

Chapter Twelve

A Taste Of Further Statistical Methods

This book is for beginners, but nevertheless a lot of useful research can be conducted with the methods discussed here. I offer here, however, a taste of what more advanced methods can do. In order not to create confusion, only a few types of test will be considered, building upon what you have already learned.

Cluster Analysis

Viewed from the perspective of a correlation matrix, the columns - the variables - were examined by way of factor analysis (we used the Principal Components Analysis technique). Factor analysis reduces the number of variables to a smaller set of underlying dimensions. In business, for example, one can work out if particular types of attitudes underlie a range of different sales figures.

Cluster analysis is another form of data reduction technique, but here the focus is upon the rows of the matrix, which represent records: observations of phenomena or the individual participants. Here, data is reduced to *objects* or groups of people. In the range of sales figures, we may discover that particular groups of people – retired or students, maybe – tend towards different purchasing patterns. So, in an inversion of factor analysis, we look not at core constructs but at the behaviour of clusters of individuals or groups of data.

Logistic Regression

At times, you are going to find that much of your research data consists of zeros and ones (yes/no). Although categorical (or qualitative) methods have their place, when you have relatively rich data sets including multiple predictors, you are likely to want to use methods which can sensitively weigh up the relative contributions of different variables. Logistic regression has a range of uses and allows the sophisticated measurement of binary data. You will find Logistic Regression in StatsDirect.

Multidimensional Scaling

MDS allows the variables of factor analysis and the objects of cluster analysis to be viewed together in interaction. This has a wide range of applications and allows both visual representation and some reflection of the magnitude of differences.

Meta-analysis

Analysis of a range of findings together. StatsDirect contains tools for this.

TALKING POINT

Although other useful tests are available, many researchers rarely operate beyond the statistical foothills. If you mastered all of the techniques in this book, which I hope proved enjoyable and useful to you, this may be all that you need; but having gained such skills, you should be able to benefit from more advanced training as required.

INDEX OF TESTS

Index of Concepts

Index of Concepts